sleuth or dare

Framed & Dangerous

sleuth or dare

Partners in Crime

Sleepover Stakeout

Framed & Dangerous

sleuth or dare

Framed & Dangerous

Kim Harrington

Scholastic Inc.

NEW YORK   TORONTO   LONDON   AUCKLAND
SYDNEY MEXICO CITY NEW DELHI HONG KONG

ISBN 978-0-545-38966-2

12 11 10 9 8 7 6 5 4 3 2 1   12 13 14 15 16/0

Printed in the U.S.A.   40
First edition, July 2012

Book design by Tim Hall

Chapter

1

A dark cloud followed me to school Monday morning. Not that I usually walked there all smiles and rainbows — I'll admit I'm not a morning person in general. But now, there was even more of a reason to feel down.

I slogged up the sidewalk alone, hoping my eyes weren't too puffy from crying. The day before, I'd had a huge argument with my best friend, Darcy Carter. We'd been joined at the hip ever since she moved to our small New England town of Danville years ago. And our lives had recently gotten a whole lot more interesting. Darcy and I had formed our own detective agency, Partners in Crime. We'd solved some cool cases and helped out fellow classmates.

But Darcy had started feeling jealous about time I was spending with other friends. And I was getting aggravated with her mood swings and her bossiness.

It came to a head yesterday in one of those horrible conversations that seem to happen so fast, you can't control the words coming out of your mouth. Pent-up feelings came pouring out. We both said things I'm sure we didn't mean (at least I didn't). And, before we knew it, we were agreeing to end our friendship and close down our detective agency.

I'd had this terrible feeling in my stomach ever since, and I spent most of last night crying. But I was also still mad at Darcy for the things she'd said.

I had no idea what today would bring. I knew we'd see each other at school, and the thought of it made me so nervous. How should I act? Should I ignore her? Try to apologize?

Normally, when I was a jumble of anxiety like this (which was often), Darcy would say, "Calm down, stress ball. Everything will be all right." But I couldn't turn to Darcy for help when she was the one I was stressed about.

"Norah! Norah!" a voice rang out.

My heart revved and I looked up, but it was only Maya Doshi. Not that I didn't like Maya. I did. But, for a second there, I had thought it was Darcy calling me. Maybe wanting to apologize and make up.

Maya started running toward me, her thick black hair held back by an orange headband. She'd moved to town this year and was a seventh grader at Danville Middle School with Darcy and me. She was super shy and had trouble making friends but, while solving a case for her recently, we'd helped bring her out of her shell.

I stopped in my tracks. Maya seemed really keyed up about something. And that wasn't the only strange thing. There were no other kids hanging around the front of the school. Where was everyone?

A minivan pulled up to the curb and I could see my classmate Abigail Mattimore in the backseat. But I watched as Mr. Hogan, the vice principal, walked up to the driver's side and said something to Abigail's mom. Quickly, the car pulled away. I blinked in confusion. What was going on?

Maya finally reached me, out of breath. "The field house . . ." she gasped, "is on fire!"

My head rocked back. "What?"

The field house was behind the school, so I couldn't see it from here. But I looked up into the sky and . . . I'd been right. A dark cloud *had* followed me to school. For real.

"You don't smell it?" Maya asked incredulously.

My nostrils twitched. Yes, there was a smoky stench to the air. I'd been so lost in my thoughts, I hadn't noticed.

"Come with me," Maya said. "Everyone's watching it."

Maya jogged off and I followed, past the main entrance and around the corner of the school. There was a large group of kids huddled together. A pillar of smoke rose into the air above their heads. The burning smell intensified. Maya grabbed my hand and pulled me through the clumps of boys and girls.

When we finally found a part in the crowd, my heart caught in my throat. It was one thing to be *told* the field house was burning. The true shock came from seeing it with my own eyes. Flames leaped out of a hole that was once a window. The air was painted in shades of orange and red. The fire sounded like a monster, making cracking, spitting noises. Two fire trucks were parked beside the building, and a long line of firemen pointed a hose at the flames.

Even as far back as we were, I still felt the heat on my cheeks. I looked around, and everyone's face mirrored the shock I felt.

Danville Middle School's gym was a notoriously nasty old place with chipped floors and ancient equipment. So the school started building a field house. A separate building that would have a shiny new basketball court, an indoor track, and pull-out bleachers for spectators. Most people were pretty excited about it. (Well, except for the soccer team. It had been built on their field, so now they had to practice at the high school.) It had almost been finished, too. They'd painted the outside red and black, our school colors. The ribbon-cutting ceremony was supposed to be in two weeks.

But now it was wrecked.

I wasn't a sporty girl at all, but I still felt a twinge of sadness looking at the charred remains of the building. I wondered what had caused the fire. Maybe something with the wiring or electricity. I remembered that had been the issue when there'd been a small fire in our neighbor's house years ago.

The smoke was making my eyes sting. I took my glasses off and held my hand up to my face for a moment. Kids in the crowd were moving around, jostling one another for a better view. And suddenly, I reopened my eyes and found myself beside Darcy.

She wore jeans and a long-sleeved black T-shirt. Her short, choppy black hair lifted in the breeze — except for the purple streak that was tucked behind her ear. Her wide brown eyes watched the flames as they licked at the sky. I opened my mouth, wanting to say something, but I didn't know what. Maybe I'd start with "hi."

But before I got the chance, I felt a rush of heat. I turned back to the fire, and it seemed to be reaching out toward us!

I staggered back a step, as did everyone else, frightened by the sudden change. But then the fire retreated again. The wind had changed direction, that was all. But it clearly wasn't safe here. I turned to check on Darcy, but in the place she'd been standing I saw only orange embers floating in the air. I gazed around, and there she was, off by herself, taking pictures with her phone.

I crossed my arms. She hadn't even said a word to me. But, then again, I hadn't spoken to her, either.

I sighed. This was so hard.

"Students!" Principal Plati bellowed over the crowd. He cupped his hands around his mouth like a bullhorn. "School is canceled! Please head to the school lobby for dismissal!"

A few kids whooped and clapped, but most remained subdued in shock. It's not every day that you come to school and find a building on fire. Everyone started shuffling along and I somehow found myself at the end of the crowd. I cast one last look over my shoulder at the flames and saw something that made my stomach clench.

An ambulance. It had been hidden from view by a fire truck, but now it was pulling away, lights and sirens on. Meaning someone was inside it. Hurt, maybe worse.

I'd lost sight of Maya, which wasn't hard since she's the smallest girl in the school. We all got to the lobby and listened to the principal speak. He'd been able to redirect the buses, and parents at drop-off were told to go back home. So it was only those of us that walked who needed to be dismissed and picked up by our parents.

I stood next to Hunter Fisk and Slade Durkin, two big kids who were known as our class bullies. But Darcy and I had recently made a sort of truce with them. Darcy stood on the other side of them now. Only three people away, but it felt like a mile between us. I knew her mother had longer to drive from work. I could offer to have my mom drive her home, too. . . .

"Dude, it's totally the Prom Killer back to haunt the halls again," Hunter said.

"Definitely," Slade agreed.

I narrowed my eyes. "What are you guys talking about?"

"You haven't heard of the Prom Killer?" Hunter asked.

"That's just an urban legend," Trey Watson, another boy from my grade, scoffed.

"It is not," Slade said. "It really happened, and it happened here in Danville."

I noticed Darcy had moved a couple steps closer and was listening in on the conversation. A mystery like this was totally up her — and our — alley. I met her intrigued gaze, but then she quickly looked back down at the floor.

Fine. If that was the way she wanted it. I looked straight ahead and stopped listening to Hunter and Slade. The story was probably bogus, anyway. Like the time Hunter tried to convince me that the nice old lady who lived across the street from Maya was a witch.

"Norah Burridge!" Principal Plati called out.

My mother was here. I thought one last time about offering a ride to Darcy. But instead I hitched my backpack up on my shoulder and walked out the door.

When we got home, I told my mom I was sad about the field house and went up to my room. I lay in bed and cuddled my dog, Hubble. But the real reason for my misery was that Darcy was right next door, and we couldn't hang out. Nothing felt right.

The phone rang downstairs. I stiffened, closed my eyes, and wished, *Let it be Darcy. She's sorry. I'm sorry. We'll make up. And everything will go back to normal.*

Moments later, I heard Mom's footsteps on the stairs. I sat up in bed. *Please let it be for me. Please let it be for me.*

She knocked. "Norah?"

I scrambled out of bed and dashed to the door, wiping the half-dried tears from under my eyes. I opened the door with a smile, but Mom had an unusual expression on her face.

"The phone's for you," she said.

My heart beat wildly. *Yes! The fight would be done now. I'd invite Darcy over. We'd watch TV. . . .* But then I noticed Mom was smirking. She never smirked when Darcy called. And now she was outright grinning.

As she put the cordless phone in my hand, she whispered, "It's a boy." Then she turned on her heel and went back down the stairs, giving me privacy.

I stared at the phone in my hand like it was an alien object. A boy had never called me before. I was disappointed that it wasn't Darcy. But at the same time my whole body felt electric with happiness. Was it Zane?

I thought Zane Munro was the cutest, kindest boy in my grade — maybe in the universe. I'd had a crush on him for millennia. And Maya had told me yesterday that, miracle of miracles, Zane liked *me*, too.

Was he calling to *tell* me he liked me?

There was only one way to find out.

I slowly put the phone up to my ear. I tried my best to hide my excitement and told myself to be cool.

"Hello?" I said. *Not bad. My voice wasn't even shaking.*

"Hi, Norah. It's Zane."

My heart shot through the roof and launched into orbit.

"Hi, Zane!" *Still in control. Still masking how happy I am.* "How are you?"

"Not good," he answered, and I realized his voice didn't sound normal. Something was wrong.

Zane cleared his throat. "I need help. I need Partners in Crime."

Chapter

2

I knocked on Zane's front door.

Yeah. That's right. I was at Zane Munro's *house*. He lived only two doors down from Maya, but I had never been inside his place. My stomach was whirling like a tornado. I reminded myself to calm down. I wasn't here to hang out. This was Partners in Crime business.

The door swung open and Zane gave me a half smile, but I could tell it was forced. The worried look in his eyes said everything.

He led me inside. "I'm sorry to make you come all the way here, but I wanted to show it to you guys in person." Then he glanced over my shoulder, doing a double take. "Where's Darcy?"

"Oh, um, she . . . couldn't come," I fibbed.

"Okay, you can fill her in." We'd reached the kitchen. It was homey and smelled like recently baked cookies. The kind of kitchen that made you feel warm inside.

"I was just about to eat a sandwich. Would you like one?" He pointed to a sandwich on a second plate. I saw the peanut butter and jelly oozing out the sides, and my stomach growled.

"Thanks," I said, sitting down. "PB&J is my favorite."

"Mine, too!" Zane said, settling in the chair beside me.

We both took bites. The silence was kind of awkward. The light chatter of a talk show leaked in from the living room where his mom must've been watching TV.

Zane wiped his mouth with the back of his hand. He was sitting so close I could've counted the freckles on his nose. (Not that I would. Okay, maybe. They're so cute!) But I forced myself to focus.

When Maya had told me that Zane liked me, too, she'd made me promise not to let him know that I knew. He had told her in secret. So I had to act like

13

everything was normal, even though, on the inside, I was exploding like a supernova.

I put the sandwich down and used a napkin to make sure I didn't have jelly on my face. "So . . . is this about your wallet?" I asked. "Did someone steal it?" That was the first thing that had come to my mind when he'd asked me to come over. I remembered him telling me yesterday that he'd lost his wallet.

Zane looked confused for a moment, then shook his head. "No, my wallet never showed up. I must've lost it. It's no biggie. I only had a couple of bucks in there, plus my student ID, which can be replaced."

"Then, what's going on?" I asked, starting to feel even more anxious.

He gazed at me, and his normally bright eyes darkened. "I think someone's out to get me."

I held back a gasp. "What would make you think that?"

"When I got home from school just now, I checked my e-mail. Someone sent me an anonymous message, early this morning."

My brain immediately went into panic mode. *No one sent him an e-mail about me, did they? About my crush on him? Or telling him not to like me? Or saying that I'm a dork and he could do better? Or . . .* My stomach clenched as I turned over the possibilities. "What did it say?" I asked.

"I can show you," he replied.

A closed laptop was centered on the kitchen table. He slid it toward us and pulled it open. The screen whirred to life. He'd left the e-mail there for me to see.

Though there wasn't much. Just one line.

YOU'LL BE BLAMED.

I felt instant relief that it wasn't about me, but that was quickly replaced with confusion. "That's it?"

Zane nodded.

"Blamed for what?" I asked.

"I don't know. It's kind of creepy, don't you think?"

I checked out the sender. I didn't recognize the e-mail address and it wasn't even a name or anything. Anonymous, like Zane had said.

I cleared my throat. "Okay, first things first. Did you try responding to the e-mail?"

"Yeah," he said. "Right away. But no one wrote back."

15

"Maybe it's nothing," I said hopefully. "Maybe someone sent you the e-mail as a joke. Like a prank from one of your friends on the soccer team."

"I really hope so. But the only way to know for sure is to find out who sent it." He paused and smiled sheepishly. "That's where you come in. I know Partners in Crime has solved mysteries even harder than this. It should be easy, right? Will you and Darcy take on my case?"

I grimaced. Truth time. "Darcy and I are . . . not speaking right now."

"What?" Zane blurted, shocked. "You guys are always together! You've been best friends for years."

This intense meeting with Zane had temporarily pushed out the sadness I felt about my fight with Darcy. But now it was back.

Darcy had said Partners in Crime was "over," but here was someone who really needed the agency's help. Could I take on the case without Darcy? I didn't know. I'm smart, but Darcy's the technology pro. She has special software and computer stuff that can figure out things I'd never be able to. Like who sent that e-mail.

Panic started to creep into the back of my mind. I dropped the rest of my sandwich, not hungry anymore. I looked up into Zane's blue eyes. I couldn't let him down. Not when he could be in real trouble.

Focus, Norah, I told myself. *You can do this.*

"My fight with Darcy is complicated," I said. "But don't worry. I'll help you myself."

On Tuesday morning, we were told to skip homeroom and head directly to an assembly. I took a minute to stop at my locker and toss my backpack and jacket inside. Everyone was rushing toward the auditorium. Kids had never been this excited about a school meeting before. But they wanted details about the fire.

I was one of the last students to get to the auditorium. I walked through the doors and scanned the rows of seats, looking for any friendly face. I saw Maya, but there were no empty seats near her.

Then, two rows behind Maya, I saw Darcy. She had Hunter Fisk on one side and an empty seat on the other. Only a few weeks ago, Hunter would've been the last person on earth that Darcy would ever sit with. But he was starting to change a bit, for the better, thanks in part to the last case we'd solved.

Hunter must've said something funny because Darcy threw her head back in laughter. Then Hunter held out his fist and Darcy bumped it.

Jealousy rose up inside me. The fist bump was *our* thing. A hollow in my heart ached, the empty space where my best friend belonged.

Then Darcy noticed me, straightened in her seat, and stared. My nerves went crazy, from my stomach to my fingers, and I thought there was a real chance that I would lose my breakfast right there in front of everyone.

Then she looked away.

The seat beside her *was* empty. What would she do if I sat there? Yell at me? Ignore me? Or . . . maybe we'd make up. Maybe she felt just like I did.

I stood frozen for a moment, not knowing what to do. I decided to make a deal. If she looked at me again, I'd go over there.

Look at me. Look at me.

A voice behind me said, "Norah, over here!"

Fiona Fanning waved at me with one hand, while using the other to save the seat beside her. Fiona was the prettiest, most popular girl in school. Today, her long brown hair fell in stylish waves along the shoulders of her red cashmere sweater. Meanwhile, my dark-blond hair hung limply down the back of my gray hoodie. I was an astronomy-obsessed nerd and she was destined for the fashion runway. But we'd bonded over a Partners in Crime case and were unlikely, but real, friends.

That budding friendship had caused a rift to form between Darcy and me. But our fight also involved miscommunications and other best-friend drama. None of which was Fiona's fault.

I adjusted my glasses on my face and made my way over to the seat beside Fiona. Before I could whisper hello, Principal Plati immediately walked to the podium.

"As you all know," he began, "our brand-new field house has been destroyed. The brave firefighters did their best against the flames, but we will need to completely rebuild. The area around the field house is roped off. It is unsafe. And the fire department is investigating. So no student is allowed near what's left of the building. Is that understood?"

We all nodded.

Principal Plati cleared his throat, as if the next part was harder to say. I squirmed in my seat.

"Mr. Gray, our school janitor, was there early yesterday morning and saw the building in flames. He called 911 and rushed to the field house to try to help put the fire out with an extinguisher. Unfortunately, he was hurt and is being treated in the hospital now for smoke inhalation and other injuries."

A hush fell over the crowd. This was even worse news. The field house was just a building. It could be replaced. Mr. Gray was a person. And a nice one, at that. He always smiled and waved as you passed by. My eyes got all watery at the thought of him lying in a hospital bed. How could something like this happen?

As if he knew that would be the next question, Mr. Plati said, "We've been told from the fire department that there's a chance this was arson."

Fiona leaned in and whispered, "What does that mean?"

I knew the term from watching *Crime Scene: New York* with Darcy. "It means it wasn't an accident," I whispered back. "Someone tried to burn down the field house on purpose."

I felt eyes on the back of my head, like someone was watching me. I turned in my seat and found Zane staring at me with a worried look on his face.

Normally, I'd be excited to catch Zane staring at me. But his expression made a shudder go down my spine.

I remembered the e-mail he got.

You'll be blamed.

That didn't have anything to do with the fire . . . did it?

Chapter

Fiona and I walked out of the auditorium together. Zane had left with his soccer team friends, after giving me one last desperate look over his shoulder.

Fiona threw her hands in the air. "This is terrible!"

"I know." I shook my head sadly. "Poor Mr. Gray."

Fiona arched an eyebrow as if she'd forgotten the fact that Mr. Gray was currently in the hospital fighting for his life. "Well, yes, that's horrible, too," she said. "But I was referring to the tragedy of our new field house being destroyed."

I shrugged, not getting why she was being so over-dramatic. "They'll rebuild it."

Fiona opened her mouth wide like I'd said the

dumbest thing on earth. "Not in time! They can't build a new field house in two weeks."

"In . . . two . . . weeks?" My mind searched for what could possibly be so important to her. Fiona was a cheerleader for the football team. They played outside.

"The school dance, Norah!" she said, exasperated.

Oh. *That.* I'd seen new posters for the dance hanging in the hallway just that morning, but I hadn't given a thought to the dance yet. "It can be in the gym," I suggested.

Fiona looked offended. "That nasty old place? It smells like dirty socks!"

She started walking quickly, letting her fingers trail along the lockers. I rushed to keep up with her as she chattered on.

"I suppose you're right, though," she said. "The Dance Committee barely has enough money for decorations. We can't afford to have it anywhere off school property. We'll have to do it in the gym."

The words poured out of her mouth in a stream of anxious babbling.

"The Dance Committee is really going to need some creative ideas now. People have the most unrealistic theme suggestions, and now I have to deal with this mess." Then, like a lightbulb had lit up in her head, she stopped and pointed at me. "You."

I put a hand to my chest. "Me?"

"Yes, you."

"Me what?"

"You need to join the Dance Committee."

Did *she* have smoke inhalation? The Dance Committee was made up of all the most popular girls in school. Girls who wouldn't bother to even speak to me, never mind listen to my ideas. Fiona must have been insane. I started to back away. "Uh, no thanks. I'm, uh, busy."

"Wait." Fiona grabbed the sleeve of my hoodie. "I need you, Norah. You're smart, creative, and organized."

"But I don't really —"

Fiona started hopping in place, repeating, "Please, please, please, please, please."

"Fine, fine," I said, mainly to make her stop. "I'll go to one meeting and see how it is."

"Great!" Fiona clapped her hands together. "It's right after school in Room 111." She lowered her voice and added, "Maybe after the meeting we can talk about how to get Zane to ask you to the dance."

She wagged her eyebrows at me, spun around, and walked away.

I hadn't even thought about that as a possibility. A little grin spread across my face.

I was suddenly a lot more interested in the school dance.

After the assembly, classes were held as normal. I tried my best to focus even though I was anxious about ten thousand different things. I'm a worrier by nature, so this isn't exactly breaking news, but I didn't usually have so much to obsess about at once. The fire, Darcy, Zane, why I'd agreed to join the Dance Committee . . .

When the bell rang for lunch, I realized that I'd have to face Darcy. It was easy to ignore our fight in class. I paid attention to the teacher, as usual. But in the lunchroom we always sat together and talked. Every day. I stopped and stared at the kids rushing through the open doorway, excited to eat and join their friends. It felt like there was a giant boulder sitting in my stomach.

If I walked in and she was sitting at our usual table,

did I just go and sit next to her? Or . . . if I went in and she wasn't there yet, did I sit in our regular spot?

I didn't know what to do.

I took a deep breath and stepped into the large, noisy room. My eyes went directly to our usual spot. Maya was there, but Darcy wasn't sitting with her. Where was she? Did she make a new friend already, or was she eating alone in the library to avoid me? How could she be so cold?

My mood swung from nervous to angry. I bet Darcy hadn't even cried over our fight like I had. She never cries. Not even when she broke her arm in fourth grade. I tried to harden my heart. She's a robot. Who wants a robot as a friend anyway?

But she was also hilariously funny. And smart. And easy to talk to.

On the surface we seemed like opposites. She dressed to stand out, I liked blending in. She got in trouble so much that Principal Plati had her mother on speed-dial, and I was a goody-goody. But we did have a lot in common. We lived next door to each other. We were both only children. We were nerds and proud of it. Hanging with Fiona and Maya was fun, but no one understood me like Darcy did.

I suddenly missed her so much it felt like someone was squeezing my heart.

I had to get out of there. I spun around, left the cafeteria, and headed for the computer lab. I was pretty sure it was empty during our lunch period. I could quickly eat my sandwich and then try to get to the bottom of Zane's weird e-mail.

I peeked my head into the room. Empty. Yes! I chose the closest computer and entered my school user name and password. While it loaded I pulled my sandwich out of my paper lunch bag and took a big bite.

I'd asked Zane to forward the e-mail to me so I could take a closer look. I logged into my e-mail and clicked on the anonymous message. It had no subject line and only those three threatening words in the body. It was sent early Monday morning, when the field house was on fire. I examined the sender once more. The address was ZM at some free e-mail service. "I wonder what ZM stands for," I said, thinking out loud. But as soon as I said it, I realized those were Zane's initials.

The computer lab suddenly felt as cold as the Arctic Circle. I shivered uncontrollably. It certainly seemed like someone had created an e-mail address just to send Zane one crazy e-mail. Using his initials in the address made it even more menacing in a way. Like someone *was* out to get him.

I'd been hoping to type the person's e-mail address into Google and find some information about him or her. You never know what will pop up with an e-mail address search. But now I knew . . . this one would turn up empty. I tried anyway and got nothing.

I let out a long sigh. *Okay, Norah. What would Darcy do?*

She'd find out more about the e-mailer.

I searched "how to find out who sent an e-mail" and wasted the rest of the lunch period reading articles that made no sense to me. E-mail tracers, ISP providers, IP addresses — I didn't know what any of that meant. I ran my fingers roughly through my hair.

Totally frustrated, I logged out of the computer and threw the rest of my sandwich away.

This was going to be harder than I thought.

Chapter

4

I waited outside classroom 111, where the Dance Committee meeting was being held. It hadn't started yet, but I could hear all the squealing and chatter inside. I stood in the hall, out of sight, and nervously toyed with the end of my ponytail.

I'm not usually a big joiner, though I was, briefly, the president of the Astronomy Club. (We only had one meeting. Darcy was the sole person to show up, and that was just because she felt bad for me.)

The Dance Committee had a much bigger turnout. I took a peek through the open door, then pulled my head back out. Just as I had suspected. All the popular girls. Fiona was there, too, but that still didn't make me comfortable enough to join in.

Suddenly, an arm reached through the opening, grabbed the sleeve of my hoodie, and pulled me inside.

"Maya?" I gasped, surprised.

She stood with a sheepish grin. "I thought it would be fun to join the committee. What do you think?"

"Yeah, totally. This will be great." I said the words, but I didn't know if I believed them.

But I was glad Maya was there. When she first moved to our town a few weeks ago, she was so shy she barely spoke. Now it was clear she was becoming braver.

"Why weren't you at lunch?" Maya asked. "It was just Darcy and me at the table."

My heart skipped a beat. Darcy showed? She must've been in the lunch line when I'd looked at the table. A guilty lump formed in my throat.

"Darcy and I are, um, in a little fight," I said. I quickly summarized the implosion of our friendship, and Maya frowned.

"I'm sorry to hear that," she said softly. "I can't imagine you guys as *not* being joined at the hip." She shook her head. "Maybe that's why she seemed even moodier than usual."

Before I could dwell too much on that, Fiona waved at me from across the room. I started plowing her way through the crowd.

"I'll save you a seat in the back," Maya said, and scurried off.

"You're here!" Fiona said when I reached her. "I thought you were going to back out of your promise."

I wanted to, I thought. But I plastered on a half smile and said, "Yeah, I'm here. Ready to go."

Fiona gave a little clap. "Great. I'm sure whatever you've come up with is awesome. Here's how it'll work. When I ask for theme nominations, you raise your hand, then I'll call on you to come up to the podium and present your idea."

My mouth fell open. "I didn't know you were going to put me on the spot." I had solved some seriously creepy mysteries, including one in the woods at night in the dark, but the thing I was most frightened of was standing up and speaking in front of the class. I'd rather clean every toilet in the whole school. That's how much I hate public speaking.

"Well, duh," Fiona said. "I told you, we need creative ideas. And you're smart. I knew you'd come up with something great. You'll be fine."

I didn't want to break it to her that — between all the drama with Darcy and Zane — I hadn't *thought* about any ideas for the dance.

"You're not going to let me down, right? Amanda and Violet have the most ridiculous idea, and I don't want everyone else to just go along with them." Fiona blinked her giant green eyes at me and made a pouty face.

"Um, yeah," I said. "I won't let you down. My idea rocks."

I just had to think of one. Like now.

But it was hard to concentrate. Somebody smelled like they'd taken a bath in perfume that morning. I wriggled my nose and held back the urge to gag.

"*You're* going to the dance?" a snarky voice said over my shoulder.

Fiona took a step back to make room for Amanda and Violet to join our conversation. I knew who they were, but I didn't think they'd ever spoken to me before. They were popular, but not in Fiona's inner circle.

Amanda's long, silky black hair cascaded down one shoulder. She looked up at me with wide hazel eyes.

Everything about her seemed soft. Violet had similar hair, but it was more bluntly cut. And she had a little nose that turned up at the end, like it was disgusted with everyone.

Violet was the one who'd spoken to me, barely disguising her disbelief that I was interested in the school dance.

"Yeah," I said, trying to force confidence into my voice. "I'm going."

"With who?" Violet asked. It sounded like a challenge.

I shrugged. "I don't know yet. Maybe just with friends."

Violet smirked at Amanda. But Amanda didn't smirk back. Instead, she waited for Violet to look away, then gave me an apologetic smile. I was glad to see she wasn't as mean as her friend.

"That's cool," Fiona chimed in. "There's nothing wrong with going stag. Who needs boys?"

"Says the most boy-obsessed girl in the school," Amanda joked.

We all chuckled. The mood seemed to be lightening at least.

"Besides," Fiona said. "Like I've said before, I'm pretty sure *someone* is going to ask Norah."

Oh no. I glared at Fiona, willing her to keep quiet. I didn't want her telling everyone that Zane was going to ask me. Then what if he didn't? I'd look like an idiot. Though, it sounded like she might've already told people. I gritted my teeth.

Fiona, thankfully, understood my look and said, "Anyway, time to start the meeting!"

I sat next to Maya while Fiona confidently strode up to the podium. She pulled out a glitter-covered gavel and banged it twice. I held back a giggle, imagining what wisecrack Darcy would say about that if she were here.

Mrs. Haymon, a teacher who taught an accelerated math course I was taking, was correcting tests in the back corner. Every club has to have a teacher-advisor present at all meetings. But Mrs. Haymon didn't need to do anything to gain control of the crowd. Fiona seemed to be on top of that.

Fiona cleared her throat. "Welcome, Dance Committee members. First, whoever came in early yesterday morning and hung the posters for the dance, thank you, but it would've been better to wait until *after* we had a theme. Now we'll just have to re-hang new ones after we vote." She paused and looked around the room. "Who hung them?"

No one raised a hand. I actually didn't blame them. Who'd want to be put on the spot like that after having made a mistake?

Fiona rolled her eyes. "Okay, well, *thanks* ghost poster hanger. Moving on." She straightened her shoulders and lifted her chin. "The destruction of the brand-new field house is *not* going to ruin our dance. We'll have to have it in the old gym, yes, but we're going to have an *amazing* theme that will make up for it. Agreed?"

Everyone clapped and whooped. I was impressed. If a career in fashion didn't work out for Fiona, she could always be a politician.

Fiona banged her gavel once to silence the crowd. Mrs. Haymon called out, "Keep the budget in mind!"

Fiona nodded. "Yes. When thinking of ideas, remember our budget is small. We need something that's doable." She seemed to stare right at Violet and Amanda as she said it. Then she looked back at the rest of us. "Anyone with an idea for a theme can come up and present it. After all nominations have been heard, we'll bring it to a vote. Who wants to be first?"

Fiona looked straight at me, but I didn't raise my hand. I looked away, down at the floor, up at the lights, anywhere but back at her. Kind of like when a teacher asks a question and you don't want to be called on, and you convince yourself that you're invisible if there's no eye contact.

I was scared that she was going to call on me anyway, but then Violet shouted, "Us! Us!"

Breathing a sigh of relief, I watched Violet and Amanda approach the podium. Good. This would give me time to come up with my own idea.

Amanda stood beside but also one step behind Violet. It was clear who would be doing all the talking. Violet leaned forward and said, "What could be more thrilling than a glittery, excitement- and drama-filled . . . Hollywood theme!" She made jazz hands to emphasize her point.

The girls all around me whispered back and forth, mostly looking unsure.

Violet spoke loudly, "We would need four spotlights to spin around the room, a red carpet, and several photographers to act as paparazzi. We would need about a dozen potted palm trees."

Sheesh. Her list of ideas sounded more like demands.

She waved a finger in the air as she added, "*And* I think it would be best if we made the dance couples only. If we don't do that, the boys will just hang out with their friends. And everyone should dress up like their favorite celebrity couple."

Personally, I thought the boys would rather spend the night home with the stomach flu than attend *that* dance. But no boys were here to vote. Fiona was right. This could be a disaster.

"And for pictures," Violet said, "we'd need a huge background display that's a replica of the Hollywood sign."

While Violet continued to list off "required" items that would surely not be in our budget, I racked my brain for an idea of my own. What did I know about dances? I'd never been to one. I didn't know about anything except astronomy. I didn't belong here with these girls. I wished I was hanging out with Darcy. Or in my yard at night, gazing through my telescope, looking for . . .

Then it hit me.

I could picture it vividly in my mind. And I knew it would work.

"So, in summary," Violet said, "no idea is going to be better than ours so we should just vote now. Raise your hand if —"

Fiona stepped forward and banged the gavel. "Great job, Violet and Amanda. Anyone else?" She looked at me with pleading eyes.

I took a deep breath and raised my hand.

Fiona pretended to be surprised. "Norah Burridge! Please, come on up."

Everyone turned in their seats and watched me. My heart started beating like crazy. *You can do this*, I told myself. *Just stand up and start walking.*

A wave of nerves slammed into me as I strode up the aisle. I reached the front, turned, and faced everyone. They were all seated in desks, staring at me. Waiting. I gripped the podium tightly to hide the trembling of my hands.

"My idea, um, is . . . A Starry Night."

Violet rolled her eyes from the front row.

I took another deep breath. "Imagine dancing with

your friends or with your crush under a beautiful night sky. Decorating would be easy. Party stores sell star-shaped balloons and cutouts. We could also make our own stars and planets from cardboard and tinfoil and hang them from the ceiling. We could have glow-in-the-dark stars up on the walls. And we could even sell glow bracelets to make some money!" At this, I saw Mrs. Haymon nod encouragingly and I felt a burst of confidence. "Also," I finished, "I have a huge poster of a full moon that we could use for a backdrop for photos."

Fiona beamed proudly from the corner of the room. Girls whispered excitedly and nodded. All except Violet and Amanda.

I had to force myself to walk rather than run back to my seat. My heart started to slow back to normal. I couldn't believe I'd said all that! And it had actually made sense!

Fiona held her hand to her chest as she returned to the podium. "What a wonderful idea, Norah. Within budget, and totally romantic."

Murmurs of agreement came from the crowd. A few girls turned and smiled at me.

"Time for a vote." Fiona banged the gavel. "Raise your hand if you want the Starry Night theme."

It was nearly unanimous. I couldn't believe it. I felt the warm tingling of a blush on my cheeks.

"And now raise your hand if you want the Hollywood theme."

Violet's and Amanda's hands were the only ones in the air. They looked around and quietly pulled them back down.

"A Starry Night it is!" Fiona said. "At our next meeting, we'll make new posters and start on the decorations. Meeting adjourned!" She banged her gavel then ran up to me.

I barely had enough time to get up from the chair before she was whispering in my ear. "Awesome job! You rule!"

I felt a rush of pride. My obsession with astronomy had paid off! This had begun as a favor to Fiona, but now I was truly excited about planning the dance. I could picture it. Dim lights, surrounded by glowing stars, slow dancing with Zane . . .

I only wished Darcy had been there to share in the glory.

Fiona looped her arm through mine as we walked out together. "I knew asking you to join was a great idea."

I felt a bump on my shoulder. Violet brushed by me, rougher than necessary. "Sorry, nerd."

She said that like it was an insult, but I stood straighter. Being smart is something to be proud of.

AS Fiona and I walked down the hall, she continued to chatter about my dance idea.

"At the next meeting," she said, her green eyes twinkling with excitement, "be prepared to work. We're going to make those cool stars and planets you were talking about."

She opened her mouth to say more, but then, eyeing something over my shoulder, seemed to change her mind. "See you later, Norah!" She spun around, her long brown hair flying, and hurried down the hall.

Why is she in such a rush? I wondered.

But then I felt a tap on my shoulder. I turned and Zane was standing there, smiling at me.

Ah. That's why.

"What are you doing here after school?" I asked, blushing a little.

He pointed down at his outfit — a sweaty T-shirt and athletic shorts. "I just finished playing intramural floor hockey in the gym. Now I'm heading over to the high school for soccer practice. How about you?"

"I just got out of the Dance Committee meeting." I motioned toward the classroom.

"Interesting." He paused and shifted his weight. "Because I was hoping to run into you. I want to ask, um . . ."

His voice trailed off. I watched as he tugged on his ear, then ran his fingers through his hair. He seemed suddenly nervous. Was he . . . about to ask me to the dance?

A tingle of excitement ran through me.

"Yes?" I prodded.

He rubbed the back of his neck. "Um, so are you going to the dance?"

"Yes, I am," I answered quickly. My heart was doing cartwheels.

His cheeks turned pink. He kept looking up at me, then down at the floor, then back up again.

"Well, then," he finally said, "I was wondering if you'd like —"

"Zane Munro!"

Zane and I were both startled by the booming voice. Principal Plati was marching down the hallway toward us.

No! He was ruining my moment! Whatever it was could've waited one more minute!

Hopefully, he'd be quick and Zane and I could get right back to our conversation.

"Zane, you need to come to my office."

Or not.

Zane furrowed his brow. "Is something wrong, Mr. Plati?"

The principal looked from Zane to me. "We need to have this conversation in my office, Zane. Follow me. Now."

This seemed serious. And, clearly, it was something Mr. Plati wanted to tell Zane in private.

So, obviously, I had to eavesdrop.

After all, Zane might need my help.

As he and Mr. Plati walked toward the office, I pretended to read one of the dance posters up on the wall. The handwriting was round and looping, and a tiny heart was doodled inside all the lowercase *e*'s. Definitely written by a girl.

I looked back over my shoulder, and Mr. Plati and Zane were gone. Now was my chance. I dashed down the hall and went into the school office. The waiting area was empty, and the secretary had either gone home already or was away from her desk. The inner door to Mr. Plati's office was closed, and I snuck up to it.

I couldn't make out the words Mr. Plati was saying, but it was clear that he was using his angry voice. One that Darcy knew very well. It wasn't exactly yelling, but it was loud enough that I could quietly push the door open an inch and he wouldn't notice.

Now I could hear everything. I leaned my ear next to the crack and listened.

"And you're sure you had nothing to do with the fire?" Mr. Plati was asking Zane skeptically.

My heart sped up.

"Yes, sir," Zane answered with a tremble in his voice. "You know me. I've never been in trouble before. I would never do something like this."

"And you're saying you weren't even here early Monday morning when the fire started? You weren't in or around the field house?"

"No, sir," Zane replied. "Well, I mean, I was here at the school. But the field house was already burning."

There was a long pause. I wished I could put my eye up to the crack to see their expressions. Why didn't Mr. Plati believe Zane? Of course he had nothing to do with the fire. This was Zane we were talking about! He was one of the good kids.

My chest squeezed. Maybe someone called in an anonymous tip. The person who e-mailed Zane and said he'd be blamed. I shook my head. No. That wouldn't work. An anonymous tip is not evidence. It would be some faceless person's word against Zane's. Of course Mr. Plati would believe Zane.

"We have a problem then, Mr. Munro."

Uh-oh. You knew you were in big trouble when Mr. Plati called you *mister* or *miss*.

"What is it?" Zane asked.

I felt so bad for him, facing this all alone in there. Why would anyone want to put Zane through this?

Mr. Plati let out a long sigh, like he was deeply

disappointed. "The problem is that, in addition to setting the fire, you've also now lied to me. Because I know you were at the field house. I have evidence."

My mind scrambled. Evidence? What evidence?

I heard the squeak of a drawer opening. And the light thud of something being placed on the desk. Then I heard Zane gasp.

I couldn't take it anymore. I risked it and put my eye up to the crack.

"This was found at the scene of the crime," Mr. Plati said. "Look familiar?"

He lifted a small black item in his hand. A wallet. Zane's wallet.

I rocked back on my heels like I'd been slapped. Whoever set the fire had stolen Zane's wallet or found it after he'd dropped it. Then they put it at the scene to frame him. I was overcome with anger. My face felt like it was burning.

"Are you going to deny that this is your wallet?" Mr. Plati asked. "Because your student ID is inside."

Zane paled. "No, I mean yes, that's my wallet. But I lost that a few days ago."

Mr. Plati raised his eyebrows. "Inside the field house?"

Zane shook his head. "No. I've never been in the field house. It wasn't open yet."

"But when Mr. Gray ran in to try to stop the fire" — Mr. Plati pointed a finger at the wallet — "he found this on the floor."

"I — I — I," Zane stuttered.

I'd never heard him this nervous. My heart went out to him.

"Someone's framing me!" he blurted. "I got a threatening e-mail and everything!"

Mr. Plati leaned forward on his desk and clasped his hands. "Is that really the tactic you're going to use?"

"It's the truth," Zane said, bewildered. "Why would I burn the field house?"

Mr. Plati let out an aggravated grunt. "I overheard a conversation in the hall last week, between the soccer team and the basketball team. It seems some of you boys on the soccer team were all riled up about the field house."

Zane's face turned bright red, and he looked down at the floor. "We're just mad because the basketball team gets a brand-new field house and we're basically

47

kicked out. We used to practice here and now we have to go all the way to the high school for practices. It's not fair."

Mr. Plati nodded. "I heard that. It would've been hard not to, since you were using such a raised voice."

"We were angry," Zane muttered.

"But how angry?" Mr. Plati asked quietly. "Angry enough to 'burn the field house down'?" He used finger quotes as he said the words.

I nearly slid down to the floor in shock. He was *quoting* Zane? Zane *threatened* to burn the field house down?

Zane's shoulders shook. "I was only joking when I said that. It was just one of those things you say but you don't mean."

"That's what I assumed at the time," the principal said. "I thought to myself, 'Zane Munro is a good kid. He's angry right now and that's why these words are flying, but he certainly doesn't want the field house to burn down.'" He shifted in his seat. "But the problem is, Mr. Munro, that the field house *did* burn down. A week after you said that. And your wallet was found at the scene." He took a long pause. "Are you sure there's nothing you need to tell me?"

48

Zane's eyes were glassy. "No, sir."

Mr. Plati leaned back in his chair and pinched the bridge of his nose. "I'm disappointed in you, Zane. I hoped that you'd be honest and face what you did. You're better than this."

Zane banged his hand on the arm of the chair. "I didn't do it, Principal Plati. I swear! Someone is framing me!"

But Mr. Plati only shook his head. "I've already called your parents. They're on their way. The police will be taking over from now on. You can show this supposed e-mail to them. In the meantime, you're suspended from school and banned from school events. No soccer games. No dance."

My heart broke into a thousand pieces. Only a few minutes ago, it had seemed like Zane was going to ask me to my first dance. I'd been so excited and had so much to look forward to. And now it was all falling apart.

In a deep, sorrowful tone, Mr. Plati ended with, "And the rest depends on the results of the investigation."

Chairs scraped as they started to get up. I scurried back into the hall. Zane emerged from the office a moment later, looking stricken.

"I heard everything," I whispered.

Zane looked up at me with eyes that held no hope. "You believe me, right? I did say that about the field house, but only because I was mad. I didn't mean it. I never, ever would have done something like this."

I put my hand on his shoulder and said firmly, "I believe you. I know you didn't do this."

For some reason that made a bit of light return to his eyes. But, even still, he said, "You should go. I'm supposed to wait here for my parents. It's going to be bad when they get here."

"It's not fair!" I snapped. I chewed on my lip to fight back tears. "You didn't do it! I know you didn't. You told me on Sunday that you'd lost your wallet days before. *And* you got this e-mail from someone. Let me go in there and plead with Mr. Plati."

Zane shot out a hand to stop me. "Norah, no. Stay out of it. He might think you're helping me cover it up. I don't want you to get in trouble, too."

He wanted to protect me. That was ten thousand kinds of awesome, but I wasn't going to stand here and let this happen.

Zane's shoulders sagged. "I'm in huge trouble, Norah. I'm suspended and I might even get charged with a crime."

I clenched my fists. Not if I had anything to do with it.

Chapter

I walked home from school alone. It felt so unnatural not to have Darcy beside me, bumping my shoulder now and then as we walked. All I could think about was Zane and the fire. Who could have framed him? And why? If Darcy had been with me, that's all we would have talked about.

I let myself into my house and did homework by myself in my room. I got it done in half the amount of time without Darcy chattering on beside me, but it was much less fun. Mom called up when dinner was ready. I went down the stairs, feeling depressed. I felt worse when I smelled cooked mystery meat. I didn't care which meat it was. It wasn't pasta, so . . . blech.

I ate my potatoes and picked at the meat loaf, cutting it up and pushing it around the plate to make it look like I consumed more of it than I really had. Being a picky eater had made me a master at that. I considered it an art form. For good measure, I also slipped a few bites under the table to Hubble.

"Is something wrong, honey?" Dad asked halfway through the meal. "You seem a little sad."

I twisted my mouth, not knowing whether or not I wanted to talk about it. The person I really needed to talk to was my best friend. I felt so hopeless. I wanted to help Zane, but I didn't know where to start. I needed Darcy. I was still mad at her about certain things, but those almost seemed less important now.

Mom put her hand over mine and forced me to look into her eyes. "What is it, sweetie?"

They weren't going to give up. I might as well spill. I let out a deep breath. "Darcy and I aren't speaking."

Mom made a pouty-lipped face and patted my hand. "Oh no. I remember those days. My best friend and I had fights now and then, too."

"I don't know if this is just a 'now and then' kind of

fight, Mom. We might never be friends again." I swallowed down the lump in my throat.

Mom's expression changed from pity to concern. "I hope that's not the case."

"Same here," Dad piped up, reaching across the table to squeeze my other hand. "You and Darcy have been inseparable ever since she moved in next door. I thought you guys would be best friends till graduation day."

Mom clicked her fork against her plate as she thought. "Would you like me to call Darcy's mother?" she suggested. "Try to help?"

Oh, *please*, no. "I'm not in preschool, Mom," I snapped. "You can't just set up a playdate and make us be friends again."

Her eyes gazed down at her plate. "I know that."

I immediately felt bad for the way I'd said it. "I'm sorry, Mom. You're only trying to help. I just think this is something I'm going to have to fix on my own."

Saying it out loud gave me the confidence to do what I'd been avoiding all afternoon. I looked up at my parents. "I'd actually like to go next door and work on that now. May I be excused?"

I inched my way across the yard between our houses. The basement light was on, so I knew Darcy was down there, probably watching TV. Her finished basement was our hangout, and had been the headquarters of Partners in Crime. I went up to the basement door and stared at it. I usually just walked right in. But now . . . I felt like I should knock.

I lifted my hand, and right when I was about to beat on the wood, the door whipped open. I pulled my hand down quickly and thankfully avoided knocking on Darcy's face. That wouldn't be a great way to start this already awkward conversation.

"I saw you through the window, walking across the yard," Darcy explained. Of course she did — it was just like detective Darcy to always be on guard.

I swallowed hard. It felt like there was an apple in my throat.

In a clipped tone, Darcy added, "So what do you want?"

Make that a grapefruit.

"I . . . I . . . was hoping we could talk," I managed to say.

Darcy's face softened a bit. "Come on in."

I followed her into the finished area where she had a couch, a couple of beanbag chairs, a giant TV, and a Ping-Pong table. It was kind of chilly down here, but I was sweating. I sat on one end of the couch and Darcy sat on the other.

I took a deep breath. "Partners in Crime needs to solve one last case."

Darcy's expectant face dropped a bit, like she'd been hoping I was here to say something else. "Why should we?" she asked.

"Because this time, it's personal."

Darcy's eyes widened to the size of golf balls while I told her about the threatening e-mail Zane received, perhaps not coincidentally sent the morning the field house caught fire. And how the wallet he lost sometime last week had ended up at the crime scene. And, despite Zane's pleading that he was framed, Principal Plati didn't believe him because he had said that terrible, dumb thing the week before.

I wrapped up with, "So he's suspended now and the police are going to investigate. He could be in real trouble for this fire, Darcy."

"Not just the fire, but Mr. Gray was almost killed!" Darcy shook her head in disbelief. "That would be attempted manslaughter, I think. Zane could end up in juvie for years."

I rubbed my forehead. I didn't doubt Darcy for a second. Her obsession with crime shows made her an expert at this stuff.

"We have to find a way to save him," I said. "I know we're not . . ." I swallowed nervously. "*Us* right now. But I'm hoping we can temporarily put that aside to focus on this case."

Darcy agreed with a slow nod. "Do you still have the anonymous e-mail?"

"Yes. Zane forwarded it to me."

She handed me her laptop. "Okay, log in and bring it up. Then I'll see what my software can figure out."

It felt both strange and not-strange to be here with Darcy, getting to work on a case. Things were still tense between us, but it was a relief to just be talking again. I opened her laptop. A Word document was already up on the screen. It looked like she had started a new case file.

"What's this?" I asked, but I'd already started

reading. *The Prom Killer?* "Wait, is this what Hunter and Slade were talking about in the lobby yesterday?"

"Yeah," Darcy said. She reached over me to save the file and close it.

"What is that all about anyway?" I asked. I had to admit, I'd been a little intrigued when I overheard Hunter and Slade talking about it. No wonder Darcy had decided to look into it.

"It's one of those things where, if you ask five different people, you'll get five different answers," she said. "But the main legend is that a long time ago, somewhere around here, someone killed everyone at prom."

An involuntary shiver ran through my body.

Darcy continued, "After I heard those bozos talking about it, I decided to ask around. It might not be made up at all."

"It really happened?" I asked skeptically.

"Sometimes true crimes are the basis for urban legends and ghost stories," Darcy explained. "But the information — especially when it's old — gets passed on from person to person and the facts sort of disappear and become myth."

"How did the people at the prom supposedly die?" I asked.

Darcy looked down at her hands, then back up at me. "In a fire."

My blood ran cold. But that couldn't be true. If two hundred kids died in the same night, we would hear more about it than whispered stories.

"That's the legend, anyway," Darcy said. "But I'm looking for the truth underneath it. The real crime."

I laughed nervously. "Maybe the arsonist came back and burned down the field house."

Darcy snickered. "Or the ghosts of the Prom Killer's victims did it!"

Even though whatever happened was long ago, I was starting to get freaked out. "Let me log into my e-mail," I said, leading us back to Zane's case. I double-clicked on the anonymous message and passed the laptop back to Darcy.

She looked at it and nodded. "I'll get to work."

I was nervous, so I busied myself by flipping channels, but nothing good was on. I pressed LIST to see if Darcy had anything interesting on her

DVR, but it was only repeats of *Crime Scene: New York*. I'd complain, but my DVR at home was full of old episodes of *The Universe*. We all have our obsessions.

Finally, after several minutes, Darcy shut her laptop and leaned back against the couch cushions, a triumphant look on her face. "The address is fake," she said. "It's one of those free services. So anyone could have created it just to send the e-mail."

I had pretty much known that already. Though I sensed a "but" coming.

"But . . ." Darcy continued, "using the IP address, I was able to track the ISP and the user's location."

I rubbed my forehead. "Translation?"

With a devilish spark in her eyes, she explained, "I don't know *who* sent it. But I know *where* they sent it from."

My heart started racing. "And?"

"The e-mail was sent from our school."

After a shocked pause, I said, "Someone set the fire, dropped Zane's wallet, then went inside and e-mailed him from the computer lab?"

Darcy nodded. "That is messed up."

My chest felt tight. "We have to figure out who it is. But I don't even know where to begin."

"Let's start where we always do." Darcy reached into her backpack and pulled out the black notebook we used for Partners in Crime cases.

I was surprised she hadn't just tossed it in the trash, with how easily she'd suggested closing the agency. The fact that she'd held on to it gave me a little hope.

Darcy opened the notebook to a new page and pulled out a pen. "Suspects."

We sat silently, thinking for a few minutes, and came up empty-handed.

"I can't think of anyone who doesn't like Zane," I said. "He's just so . . . nice! He doesn't have any enemies."

Darcy tapped the pen on her chin. "But just because *he's* nice doesn't mean everyone else is. Someone out there is clearly angry at him."

"But what could they be mad at Zane for?" I threw my hands in the air in frustration.

Darcy stopped playing with the pen and stiffened.

"What?" I said, shifting in my seat. "You just thought of something."

"Not something," she said, meeting my gaze. "Someone."

I grabbed her arm. "You have a theory."

Darcy nodded. "Get to school early tomorrow morning. It's interrogation time."

Chapter 6

Things with Darcy weren't exactly back to normal. We hadn't made up. But we were at least working together on this one last case. I was glad she could put her feelings aside to help me. Zane didn't deserve what was happening to him.

As planned, I arrived at school early Wednesday morning. Darcy was already there, staring at a plaque on the wall by the gym.

I approached her. "So what's the plan?"

She started slightly, like she'd been deep in thought. "Oh. Hi. Um, they usually hang out at Hunter's locker in the morning until the bell rings for homeroom. We'll be waiting there today, and we'll ambush them."

Them, meaning Hunter and Slade. They were our top suspects as of our meeting last night, and the only people we could think of who might be holding a grudge against Zane. We'd most recently solved a case, and it had ended up involving Hunter, Slade, and Slade's older brothers. I thought we had ended things on a good note, but maybe the boys were looking for vengeance.

My eyes went to the plaque Darcy had been so entranced by. "What were you looking at?" I asked.

She ran her fingers over the letters. "Did you ever notice that this says the school gym was built in 1948?" Darcy said.

I'd walked by the plaque a million times but had to admit, I'd never stopped to read it. "Not before now. Why does it matter?"

"It's interesting because our school was built in 1938 . . ." Darcy said, trailing off to let me fill in the blank.

"They wouldn't have gone without a gym from 1938 to 1948," I said. "The gym must have been . . . rebuilt."

Darcy raised an eyebrow. "Perhaps after a fire?"

Of course — *The Prom Killer!* "But wait," I said.

"Why would the high school hold their prom at a middle school?"

Darcy grinned. It felt good to see her smile at me again, even if she was clearly just excited about the case. "Good catch. But this didn't become the middle school until the town grew and they needed a bigger high school. In 1948, our school *was* the high school."

That was right! I remembered seeing photos and trophies in the big glass case in the lobby, back from when our school was a high school. An idea came to me. "How much time do we have?"

Darcy glanced down at her watch. "They should be getting here any minute. Why?"

"I want to make a quick detour."

I hoped it was still there. I led Darcy down the main hall and toward the giant glass case. It took up almost the entire wall and was full of trophies and plaques from years past. One of the more eye-catching displays was a giant poster with small photos showing each year's prom king and queen. I remembered Fiona once laughing at some of the styles of decades past.

I put my hands up to the glass. "It's still here."

"What?" Darcy said, but then she noticed it.

The most recent prom king and queen photo was from 1964. That was the last prom held here before they built the high school. The prom queen wore a frilly, long dress and white gloves and the king had a skinny black tie. In the '50s the prom kings had white tuxes, and the girls wore dresses I'd only seen in those black-and-white movies on TV, with big puffy skirts and ribbons around their waists.

My eyes searched backward each year: 1951, 1950, 1949, 1947 . . . I stopped.

Darcy must have seen it at the same time. "Nineteen forty-eight isn't there," she said.

"They had no prom king and queen in 1948." I looked at Darcy. "The Prom Killer story might be real."

The sound of kids' footsteps dragged us out of our trance, and we remembered why we'd come to school early in the first place.

"We have to get to Hunter's locker for the ambush!" Darcy said, and broke into a jog. I followed, thoughts of the Prom Killer swirling through my head, and we were at his locker only a minute later.

Darcy straightened. "Here they come."

I wrung my hands nervously. I was all for getting answers, but I wasn't good at the confrontational stuff.

"Hey, jerks, come here!" Darcy called.

She didn't have much of a problem with confrontation.

Slade rolled his eyes, and he and Hunter sauntered over. They were both equally tall and broad-shouldered, the biggest kids in our grade, but you could always tell who was who from a distance because of their hair. Slade had a buzz cut. Hunter had a big mop of black hair that hung down so far it almost covered his eyes.

"What?" Slade snapped.

Darcy stepped forward. "We need to talk to you."

Hunter looked at Darcy with a confused expression. Maybe even a little hurt. "I thought we had a truce."

"Funny," Darcy said. "So did we."

I cleared my throat. It was easier for me to explain why we were there rather than get up in their faces like Darcy was. "Zane has been framed for the field house fire. Someone dropped his wallet at the scene and e-mailed him, telling him he'd be blamed. He's been suspended. The police are getting involved and everything."

"And so," Darcy cut in. "The only people we could think of who might want to do something like this to Zane would be . . ."

Slade tilted his head, trying to figure things out.

But Hunter cried, "Us? You think *we* set the fire in the field house and framed Zane?"

Darcy crossed her arms over her chest. "That's what we're asking."

Slade shook his head. "It wasn't us."

"No way," Hunter insisted. He roughly shook the hair out of his eyes. "Maya can vouch for me. I walked to school at the same time she did Monday morning. The field house was already on fire when we got there."

I was surprised by how angry he looked. He seemed almost as mad as I was.

Hunter took a few deep breaths and his face reddened. "Look," he said. "I used to think Zane was nothing but a goody-goody teacher's pet."

"Don't hold back," Darcy quipped.

"But I've gotten to like the kid," Hunter continued. "Slade and I don't want revenge. We're thankful he — and you — helped us."

"What about . . . the others?" I asked, meaning — for the most part — Slade's nasty older brothers.

Slade's mouth turned down. "No. They're not out for vengeance either. They're scared of you guys."

My eyebrows rose. "Us?"

"Yeah," Hunter said. "After you found out their secret with your last case, they just want to lie low for a while. It's not them."

Which made sense, but left *us* . . . without a suspect.

By lunchtime, tons of people were whispering about Zane's suspension. He'd told a few of his friends, we'd told Hunter and Slade, and the news grew from there. I imagined Zane at home, all alone in his room, looking depressed and hopeless. My heart ached.

I'd tried to call him the night before, but his mom answered and said he wasn't allowed to come to the phone. Not only was he suspended, he was majorly grounded. No phone, no e-mail, no nothing. And I felt useless because I had no idea what to do next.

I brought my tray over to our usual table and sat down with a sigh. It was pasta day, my favorite, but I just pushed the spaghetti around with my fork. I wasn't hungry.

Darcy slumped down beside me and tore open her brown bag. "This stinks," she muttered. "I've been running over everything in my head. We need a clue. But we have nothing."

I grumbled in agreement. I should've at least been happy that Darcy was sitting with me, like old times, but I reminded myself that things weren't back to normal. We were only sitting together for the sake of the case.

Mrs. Wixted, our school librarian, came over to the table with a bright smile. "Hey, girls."

"Hi, Mrs. Wixted," I answered gloomily. "Are you a lunch monitor today?"

"No, I'm actually here for Darcy."

Darcy looked up from her sandwich.

Mrs. Wixted said, "I found out the answer to that question you asked me yesterday about the Danville newspaper. The town public library has it on microfilm. So you'll be able to find old copies there."

"Thanks," Darcy said and took a bite.

Mrs. Wixted scrunched up her forehead, probably wondering why we were both so miserable today. Then she shrugged and walked off.

"What's a microfilm?" I asked.

"It's a machine," Darcy said around a mouthful of turkey on wheat. She finished chewing, then added,

"Some really old newspapers aren't online, so they have scans of them. Like little photo negatives. And you put it in the microfilm machine, which blows it up big like a projector, and then you can read it."

Still confused, I asked, "Why do you want to read old Danville newspapers?"

"Research for the Prom Killer," she answered. She gazed down at her sandwich. "I don't have to work on that case, though. Not now that Zane's in so much trouble."

Strangely, I kind of wanted to work on the old case, too. I was intrigued. And I could tell that Darcy was getting totally obsessed. We could work on both mysteries. Plus, if she was making a semi-truce with me to help Zane, I could do the same for her and help with the Prom Killer case. And maybe, as we spent more time together, we'd find a way back to being friends.

"No, let's do it," I said. "We can head to the library after school. Who knows, maybe researching that old case will give us an idea for how to help Zane."

Maya laid her tray down across the table from me. "Gosh," she said. "I was last in line for the hot lunch and now I'll barely have enough time to finish it."

It looked like Maya hadn't heard about the latest development. She gazed at Darcy, then at me, and asked, "What?"

Darcy asked, "Monday morning, did you see Hunter walking to school?"

Maya thought for a moment as she unfolded her napkin. "Yeah. That was the morning of the fire. He was walking in front of me, I think. And then we got to the school and saw the flames."

"Did you see Slade?" I asked.

She chewed on her lip and looked up at the ceiling, trying to remember. "Yeah, he got there right after us. Then you came and I waved you over."

So it was true. Hunter and Slade were innocent. Darcy and I shared a look.

It stunk that we had no leads, but at the same time I was glad Hunter and Slade weren't guilty. Maybe there was hope for them yet.

"I figured it wasn't Hunter," Darcy said. "He's . . . not so bad."

I slowly blinked. Twice. Darcy had never said anything even slightly positive about that boy before. Interesting.

Maya said, "What's with all the questions?"

"It's Zane," I said sadly. "He's been suspended."

Maya gasped and dropped her fork. "What for?"

While I filled her in on the details, she covered her mouth with both hands. Zane had been so kind to her. He lived a couple houses down. When she first moved in, Hunter had started teasing her while they walked home from school. So Zane began walking with her so Hunter would leave her alone.

Tears formed in the corners of her eyes. "Why would someone do that to Zane? Everyone likes him."

"I don't know," I said. Thoughts churned in my head as I studied the crowd in the cafeteria. The e-mail had been sent from the computer lab. It must have been one of our classmates. But who?

My eyes went from table to table, watching people eat and chat with their friends. I scanned each face and stopped when I got to Violet. She was scowling at me from across the room.

Sheesh! What was her problem? She really had to get over this Dance Committee thing.

"Well, the good news," Maya piped up, "is that Mr. Gray is awake and he's going to be fine."

I turned back to Maya and sighed in relief. The school janitor was such a nice man. I was glad he was going to be okay.

"How do you know that?" Darcy asked, one eyebrow raised.

Maya spun long strands of spaghetti around her fork. "My aunt works at the hospital."

"Has he been released?" I asked. For the first time today, my voice had a hint of hope instead of gloom. Darcy and I exchanged a look, totally thinking the same thing. Mr. Gray might have seen something that could help us prove Zane's innocence.

Maya dabbed at her mouth with a napkin. "No, he's still in the hospital, but he's going to be all right. He's just recovering from smoke inhalation and a sprained ankle."

"Do you think your aunt could get us in to see him?" Darcy asked with a gleam in her eye.

Maya looked at the both of us, catching on. "I'll ask."

The bell rang, signaling the end of lunch, and I'd only eaten two bites. But now that we had a lead I was hungry again. I shoveled two giant forkfuls of pasta into my mouth.

"I'll catch up with you later," Darcy said. "Remember — the library after school." She didn't say it in her regular breezy tone. It was more business-like. Yet another reminder that we were just working together.

After Darcy left, I scarfed down one more big bite of pasta. Maya was staring at me.

I wiped my mouth and stood. "I know, I'm acting like a pig. But I hadn't eaten at all and then —"

"It's not that," Maya said. She stood up and carried her tray to my side of the table. She looked around suspiciously, then back at me. I saw her swallow. She was clearly nervous and trying to decide whether to tell me something.

"What, Maya? If you know something, please tell me," I pleaded.

"It's not something I know. It's just something I thought of. But it's probably not true." She shook her head. "No, it can't be."

"What?" I said loudly.

"Are you and Darcy not in a fight anymore?" she asked, her eyes anxious.

It pained me to answer. I sighed. "Well, no . . . we're still technically in a fight, I guess. We were only sitting together because we're working on Zane's case."

"And you weren't speaking Monday morning, when the fire happened."

I frowned and gripped the tray tighter in my hands. "No, we weren't. Why?"

"You don't think . . ." She hesitated, not meeting my gaze.

My mouth dropped open. "You think *Darcy* framed Zane?"

Maya's eyes widened and she whispered, "Shh. No. I'm just saying, maybe it's a possibility. You guys had your big blowup on Sunday, and then Monday morning this happens. The timing is weird, is all I'm saying. Maybe she was really mad and did something stupid and now she regrets it."

I stood, speechless, and watched Maya return her tray. I thought back to the day I had argued with Darcy. She had been mad at me because she felt like I was forgetting about her and spending too much time with new friends. I'd happily gone to her house to tell her the good news — that Zane liked me. But that made her even angrier. She'd snapped back something sarcastic, like, "Great, now you can go off and be boyfriend-girlfriend with him and ignore me even more."

And then the fire happened the next morning. And Zane had been framed.

I felt like a giant weight was being lowered onto my chest. Darcy had a bad temper, I knew that. And she'd gotten in trouble quite a bit at school. But she would never have done something like this.

Would she?

Chapter

7

Later that day, I followed Darcy through the door into the Danville Public Library. My thoughts were churning. I had no evidence that Darcy had anything to do with the fire. But Maya's words kept ringing in my head.

It's a possibility.

It's a possibility.

It's a possibility.

I shook my head roughly.

"Are you okay?" Darcy said, eyeing me strangely.

"Yeah. Just a little . . . headache," I lied.

She gave me a worried look. "Do you want to go home? We could do this tomorrow afternoon."

Here she was, being all concerned and nice, even

though we hadn't officially made up. And meanwhile I was suspecting her of arson.

I waved my hand. "I'm fine. Let's start the research."

"Oookay," Darcy said, and started walking toward the reference desk.

I steered my thoughts away from the fire and toward the Prom Killer.

The reference librarian was typing on the computer. Her hair was a pretty shade of red and held up in a tortoiseshell clip. A pair of glasses perched so low on her nose, I wondered how they stayed there without falling off.

Darcy coughed into her hand.

"Oh!" The librarian gazed up from the computer and looked at us over the rim of her glasses. "I didn't even see you two there. How can I help you?"

Darcy said, "Our school librarian said that you have old copies of the *Danville Reporter* here. On microfilm?"

The librarian raised her eyebrows in surprise. "We don't get too many people your age coming in here to use the microfilm." She got up and walked around the desk. "Was there any specific time period you were looking for?"

I stood with my hands clasped, letting Darcy do all the talking. This was her thing. I was sure she'd already figured out what papers she needed to look in.

"Spring 1948," Darcy answered quickly.

The librarian nodded. "Okay. You girls get settled downstairs, and I'll bring you the rolls."

Darcy and I looked at each other. *Rolls? Downstairs?*

At our confused expressions, the librarian said, "I take it you've never used microfilm before."

"No," I said, almost apologetically.

She pushed her glasses up on her nose and smiled. "It's no problem. I'll show you how it works. The machine is in the basement."

I'd never been in the library's basement. In fact, I hadn't even known there *was* one. But we headed in the direction the librarian had pointed and, sure enough, there was a darkened stairway in the back corner of the library.

"Looks creepy," Darcy said.

I'd been thinking the same thing, but shook it off. I reached out and flicked a switch on the wall. The stairwell lit up with a dim yellow glow.

"See?" I said. "It's fine."

Darcy nudged me with her shoulder. "You first, then, Bravey McBravepants."

I grabbed the wooden railing tightly as I descended the creaky stairs. Darcy kept close behind. The basement air was musty.

As I stepped off the bottom step, I squinted through the dim light at the shadows. It was eerily quiet. Large filing cabinets lined one wall. Beneath a dangling light-bulb stood a table, two chairs, and a big gray machine.

"That must be the microfilm machine," I said, pointing.

"People must hardly ever use this," Darcy said, wiping a layer of dust off the top.

"Here you go!"

I jumped as the librarian swiftly entered the room. She stretched out her hand toward us. It contained something that looked like miniature versions of the rolls of old camera film.

"How do you load it?" Darcy asked, taking it from her.

"You two sit down and I'll walk you through it," she said.

Darcy and I followed her directions as she explained what to do. "Put the roll onto the spindle. Now push it in hard. Great. Pull the tray out. Now thread the film under the glass. Stick it into the other reel and roll it to make sure it's secure."

I was trying hard to memorize each step in case we needed to do it again with another roll.

"Wonderful," she said. "Now turn on the machine."

I leaned forward and pressed the power button. The microfilm machine whirred to life and a bright light illuminated the glass on the tray. An old newspaper article came up on the screen.

The librarian pointed to a knob. "Now just turn the dial until you find a story you want to read. Then you can zoom in and focus to make it easier to read."

"Okay," Darcy said, sounding more confident than I felt. "Thanks."

The librarian gave us a little wave. "I'll be upstairs if you need anything. Return the rolls to me when you're done."

Now that we had privacy, I asked Darcy, "Isn't this going to take forever?"

Darcy fiddled with the dial, trying to bring the grainy black-and-white newspaper print into focus.

"Hopefully not. We know prom takes place in the spring. So we just have to look through April, May, and June 1948."

A blur of articles went by. Now and then Darcy slowed, squinted, then continued turning.

"Still," I said skeptically. "Three months?"

Darcy continued to turn the knob. "It was a weekly paper, so we only have four issues in each month. And something like this would be a big story with at least one photograph. Probably on the front page."

She was right. I sat back and tried to stop my eyes from glazing over as we examined each issue in April. There was no mention of anything related to a prom. We worked together to unload the film and reload the roll for May. We flipped through the first week. Then the second. Then the third.

I started to get a little worried that we wouldn't find anything at all.

But then Darcy jolted in her seat. I blinked and forced my tired eyes to focus on the screen. And there it was. My jaw dropped.

PROM NIGHT DISASTER

The headline was huge, and underneath was a black-and-white photo showing the ruins of the school's original gym. Girls in fancy dresses and boys in tuxes huddled together. A caption beneath the photo read: "The scene of the fire where prom festivities turned deadly."

Goose bumps raced down my arms. It *was* real. The gym had burned down on prom night.

"Where's the rest of the article?" I asked. The grainy photo took up most of the page.

Darcy rolled the dial a bit and there it was, in smaller print. She fiddled with the focus until it came clearly into view.

```
Arson is being blamed for a fire
at the high school in Danville
that left one teen dead and several
injured. Someone started the May
29 blaze at about 9 P.M., at the
Danville High School gym on Main
Street, according to the police.
Because it was prom night and the
room was filled with highly flam-
mable decorations, what began as
```

a small fire quickly spread to engulf the entire gymnasium.

Most of the partygoers were able to leave unharmed. The few injuries sustained were caused by the panic of one hundred students rushing to the doors at once. High school senior Charles Austin, the last person inside the gymnasium, lost his life. Reports say he was refusing to leave until he found and saved the life of "his girl." However, his date was already waiting safely outside.

Danville Public School officials told the paper they were still determining how much the rebuild would cost. Anyone with information on the fire is urged to call the Danville Police Department.

"Is there anything else written about it?" I asked. "This is the last week of May."

Darcy quickly unloaded the May film and I loaded

the one for June. Darcy flipped to the first week and the story was on the front page again. "Here."

PROM NIGHT DISASTER
REMAINS UNSOLVED

```
Danville authorities said they
are still investigating the prom
night arson that left one student
dead and several people injured.
They have no leads and are pleading
with the public.
    "If you know anything, please
come forward," Police Chief Micucci
said.
```

I stopped reading and leaned back in my chair. The story of the Prom Killer was based on truth. Except, instead of a crazy psycho who killed *everyone* at prom, only one person had lost his life. But it was clear the arsonist had never been caught.

"If the case was solved," I mused out loud, "there would have been an end to it. It never would have become legend."

"Right," Darcy agreed, shutting the microfilm machine off. "The story took on a life of its own and grew and grew because the town never had closure. They never got answers."

I gave her a sidelong look. I knew this wasn't the end for her. I felt like I needed to know, too. I was hooked. "What's next?" I said.

Darcy smiled, happy that I was still coming along for the ride. "I think we should find out more about Charles Austin, the only person who died. And I know just where to start."

Chapter
8

The next day at school, word about the Prom Killer spread like . . . well . . . fire. One minute Darcy was telling Fiona the true story behind the urban legend. And the next minute the whole school knew. That's sometimes a side effect of telling Fiona something.

So, of course, everyone was whispering about the ghost of Charles Austin coming back and burning the field house.

I was searching through my locker for my math textbook. I had study period next and wanted to get a head start on my homework. Violet and Amanda were in the hall, stopped outside a classroom. Violet was going on and on, trying to scare anyone who would listen.

"The ghost of Charles Austin decided that, if he couldn't have his dance, no one could!" Violet said with feverish delight. "Or maybe it wasn't the ghost of Charles Austin. Maybe it's the Prom Killer himself! He could still be alive. Or maybe . . . he's one of the undead."

Amanda's eyes widened, and she took a big step back. I didn't blame her. Violet was enjoying this scary story a bit too much. Despite how unrealistic it was.

I muttered sarcastically, "And did the Prom Killer plant Zane Munro's wallet at the scene to frame him?" It was one of those times when my brain formed a thought and it came out of my mouth before I could stop it.

Violet whipped her head around. "Are *you* talking to *me*?"

I cleared my throat, feeling nervous. "I'm just saying . . . someone put Zane's wallet there. A ghost or some old killer would have no grudge against Zane."

Violet cocked her head to the side. "And why are you so sure Zane *didn't* do it?"

I opened my mouth to explain that I'd been with him on Sunday when he realized his wallet was gone. But Violet stormed away before I had the chance to speak.

Amanda stepped closer to me, her long black hair hanging like a curtain over half her face. My stomach clenched. I didn't want to be yelled at by her, too. One popular girl tantrum per day is my limit.

"Sorry about Violet," she said softly. "She gets over-dramatic sometimes."

She was apologizing? "Uh, thanks," I said, half in shock.

"For what it's worth," Amanda continued, "I think Zane's innocent, too. I'm sure he didn't mean for any of this to happen." She was whispering, like she didn't want anyone to hear.

"Amanda!" Violet shrieked from farther down the hall. She'd probably just realized that Amanda hadn't stormed off with her.

"Coming!" Amanda called, running.

Darcy strolled up to me with an unreadable expression on her face. "Planning the dance with your new pals?"

I ignored the taunt behind her comment. Arguing wouldn't help us solve either case. "No. They're not my friends," I said, still turning over Amanda's words. "You've gotten the whole school in a tizzy about the Prom Killer." I yanked my math book free from the pile and used my elbow to close the locker door.

Darcy softened. "Speaking of . . . you have study period in the library now, right?"

I pulled my books up to my chest and asked suspiciously, "Yeah, why?"

Darcy grinned. "Because we're going to say hi to Charles Austin."

Thankfully, she didn't mean the ghost of Charles Austin, but you never knew when dealing with Darcy.

Study period in the library was supposed to be silent, but Mrs. Wixted was pretty cool and didn't mind if you whispered. So, when Darcy led me to the back corner of the library, I said, "What are we doing?"

Darcy whispered back, "Finding Charles."

The tall bookcase in the rear of the library contained all the yearbooks, dating back to when our school used to be the high school. As in . . . 1948. I realized this as Darcy ran her fingers along the books' spines. She stopped at 1948, said, "Bingo," and pulled the yearbook out.

She handed it to me as we sat at the nearest table. I cracked open the book, sending a plume of dust into the air.

"He should be near the front," Darcy whispered.

"I know how alphabetical order works," I said back. But before we even got to the regular pages of photos, there was a full-page spread devoted to the life of Charles "Charlie" Austin. The words *In Memoriam* were centered at the top.

My chest tightened as I stared wistfully at the photos. He was tall and had dark hair and the kind of smile that reached all the way to his eyes. In other words, this dude from 1948 was totally cute. And, clearly, popular. The list of clubs and sports he was involved with went on and on.

"Quite the joiner, huh?" Darcy said.

I flipped to the superlatives page and his face was all over that, too. Charlie had been voted "best looking," "most popular," and "most likely to succeed." We found his individual photo in the seniors pages, but nothing about it gave us any clues.

Darcy chuckled. "Look. All the girls have the same hair."

I flipped through the pages, and she was right. All the girls' hairdos were short with no bangs and wavy curls. The boys' hair was all slicked to the side, and they wore shirts with big collars. One even had a bow tie! Darcy and I giggled and pointed at the old-fashioned looks until suddenly a name made me stop.

"John Wolfson," I said, pointing at a skinny young man. "I wonder if that's Mrs. Wolfson's husband."

Mrs. Wolfson was an old lady who lived on Maya's street. After her husband died many years ago, she let her yard overgrow, and house repairs didn't get done. She barely left the house and earned the reputation from kids in the neighborhood as being a witch. Darcy and I found out that wasn't true at all. In fact, she was very kind. And we helped clean up her house and yard. Hopefully the kids didn't call her names anymore.

Darcy looked closer at the photo. "Mrs. Wolfson

said they were high school sweethearts, so she'd be in here, too. But I don't know her maiden name."

"Her first name is Dolores," I said. "How many of them could there be?"

We flipped through and found two, but one was clearly our Dolores. I recognized the oval shape of her face and her big, round eyes.

"Dolores Gensler," Darcy read out loud. "That's her all right."

My skin prickled. "That means Mrs. Wolfson was in the Class of 1948. She knew Charles Austin. She was probably there, that night, at prom."

I looked at Darcy.

She looked at me.

And, at the same time, we said, "Field trip!"

Apparently our BFF telepathy still worked, even if we were no longer officially BFFs.

Chapter

9

After the last-period bell rang, I hurried to my locker. Darcy and I were planning a little trip to Mrs. Wolfson's house to find out more about Charles Austin. I felt so hopeless with Zane's case. We didn't have any leads. So at least I could research the Prom Killer case and keep my mind busy.

Darcy came over, pulling her arms through her backpack straps. "Ready to go?"

"There you guys are!" an exasperated voice called out.

Maya ran up, out of breath.

"You were looking for us?" I asked.

"Yeah. You rushed out of class so quickly." She took a moment to catch her breath, then smiled at us. Like she had a secret. She whispered, "I researched the thing you wanted me to ask about, and the answer is yes, but you might have to come up with a story."

I had no idea what she was talking about.

"Mr. Gray?" Darcy guessed.

Oh!

"Yes," Maya said. "My aunt says you can talk to him in the hospital this afternoon."

I pumped my fist. "Yes!" Finally, a step forward on Zane's case.

Darcy frowned. "But we'd have to postpone our visit to Mrs. Wolfson."

"Worth it," I replied. Zane came before the Prom Killer.

"Here's the thing, though," Maya said. "Visiting hours end before my aunt's shift starts. So she can't get you in."

"So how *can* we get in?" I said anxiously. We needed Mr. Gray. He was our only lead.

Maya shifted her gaze to me. "It's family only. So you'll have to . . ."

"Go undercover," Darcy finished with a gleam in her eye.

The Danville Regional Hospital is small, and serious cases get shipped to the Boston hospitals. But, thankfully, Mr. Gray's injuries were not severe. He would actually be released soon. But we needed to talk to him ASAP. The more time went on, the more the focus would be on Zane and not on catching the real criminal.

So Darcy and I spent the afternoon biking to the hospital. It was on the opposite end of town, and by the time we got there, we were tired and covered in sweat. If we hadn't been fighting, we would have been talking and joking the whole time, so the ride would have flown by. Now, though, there was a tense silence.

Darcy wiped her brow with her forearm. "Mr. Gray had better have a lead for us after all that," she complained.

I ignored her. We chained our bikes and walked toward the main entrance. The building looked like a LEGO: brick and square, rising only three floors up. The doors whooshed open automatically, and we walked in.

"What now, you think?" Darcy asked, looking around.

My dad had to have his appendix removed a couple years ago, and I vaguely remembered the visiting process. I pointed at an oversize information desk. "We go up there and ask for his room number."

The man behind the desk looked young and bored. He was flipping through a magazine and chewing on a wad of gum. We weren't allowed to have gum in *school*, so I thought that must be against some rule in a *hospital*.

Darcy strode up to the desk confidently, her chin jutted out, her shoulders straight. "We're here to visit our uncle, Mr. Gray."

Oh, man. That sounded so weird only using a last name. What niece referred to her uncle as Mister Last Name? I braced myself for something bad. He was going to demand to see identification or proof of some kind, I just knew it. He started typing something into the computer, and I was convinced it was a secret message to security. Something like: *Imposters! Come throw them out!*

But he only snapped his gum and said, "Room 303." He aimed a thumb over his shoulder and added in a monotone, "Take the elevator to the third floor. The nurses' station will be right there. You can ask them or follow the signs."

"Thanks," I said, hurrying away.

When we got out of earshot, Darcy pumped her fist. "That was easy!"

"So far," I reminded her. "Don't jinx it. We still have to get past the nurses' station."

We found the elevator bank, and I pressed the UP button.

Darcy tapped her foot. "I hope he has some clues for us. Otherwise we —"

Over Darcy's shoulder, I saw a tall man walking our way. I held my finger to my lips, and Darcy stopped talking. The elevator dinged, and the doors opened. I tried not to look at the stranger. I felt like my guilt was written all over my face. In all caps. I AM VISITING SOMEONE AND I'M NOT A FAMILY MEMBER.

Okay, it's not the world's biggest crime. But still.

He stepped into the elevator with us, carrying a huge "Get Well" display with flowers and balloons. We only had to go up a couple floors but, since we were all silent, it seemed like the longest elevator ride ever.

Finally, it reached the third floor and the doors opened. The man walked out first . . . right to the nurses' station.

He muttered, "Delivery for Room 306."

The nurse behind the desk replied, "You can leave it here, and I'll bring it down to the room. Where do I sign?"

Darcy grabbed the sleeve of my sweater. "Now's our chance," she hissed. "Go fast!"

I followed her, quietly speed-walking past the desk. The nurse was looking down as she signed the delivery man's paperwork. We were going to make it! I looked up at a room number as we passed: 301. Mr. Gray's room was next. Almost there.

"And where are you going?" a woman's voice rang out.

Or not.

We skidded to a stop and turned around. The nurse had spotted us. The delivery man grabbed his paperwork and walked off, his job done.

"Room 303?" I answered, though it sounded like a question.

The nurse examined us closely. She was a tired-looking woman with frizzy gray hair. "Are you family members?" she asked.

"Yes," Darcy piped up. "We're Mr. Gray's nieces."

Darcy and I looked about as related as an apple and a sneaker. But maybe the nurse would buy it.

She narrowed her eyes. "Do you have an adult with you?"

Darcy and I exchanged a glance. I had no idea what to say. My brain was like an upside-down turtle, kicking frantically but getting nowhere. Darcy opened her mouth, readied with what I imagined would be a great story, but the nurse held up her hand.

"Nice try, girls," she said. "I don't know why you want to visit with your school janitor, but you'll need a family member with you to do so."

My mouth went dry. She was Psychic Nurse. We were busted. Shoulders sagging, we trudged back over to the elevator and pressed the DOWN button.

"Now what?" I whispered.

"We wait for the elevator," Darcy said sarcastically.

"And then what?"

But Darcy's eyes got big. "Shh," she said. "Wait a second."

I looked back over my shoulder and saw that the nurse was walking down the hall with the giant flower and balloon arrangement the delivery man had brought.

"As soon as she enters that room," Darcy said. "Run."

I was about to list all the reasons why this was a bad idea, but then the nurse disappeared into Room 306, and Darcy took off running. I followed, as hard as my legs would go. My heart was thudding. Only seconds later we were inside Room 303.

We'd made it!

But Mr. Gray wasn't in the bed.

A bald man, much bigger and older than Mr. Gray lay sleeping in front of us.

Darcy turned to me. "What the — ?"

But my eyes went to the yellow curtain by the side of the man's bed. It was a shared room. My dad had had one of those, too. I quietly slid the curtain aside and there was Mr. Gray, in the second bed, reading a book.

His usually clean-shaved face had stubble, and his black hair stuck out at all angles. But he didn't look too bad. His eyes widened at the sight of us.

Darcy immediately went to his bedside. "We're not supposed to be here so please talk quietly," she begged. "We want to ask you about the fire. And we're kind of in a rush."

Mr. Gray smirked and laid his book down. "Norah and Darcy. Since when did you two join the police force?"

"We just have a few questions," I said, wringing my hands. "It will only take a minute."

"I already told the police everything, girls. You should leave this to them."

Darcy said, "But our friend is the main suspect right now and we know he didn't do it."

Mr. Gray frowned. "Who?"

I couldn't hide the desperation in my voice when I answered, "Zane Munro."

The shock showed all over Mr. Gray's face. He shook his head. "Zane's a good boy. He would never do something like this."

"We know," Darcy said. "But whoever did left Zane's wallet at the scene. They framed him. This person is definitely dangerous. Who knows what they'll do next, especially with our big dance coming up. We need to figure out who it is."

"Is there anything you can remember?" I prompted. "Something you saw or heard?"

Footsteps sounded outside the door, and we all went silent. The nurse was walking from Room 306 back to her desk. I closed my eyes and hoped she didn't stop to check on the patients in here. I stood completely still, every muscle in my body frozen.

The footsteps passed.

I exhaled in relief. "Please," I said, begging Mr. Gray with my eyes.

He let out a long, slow breath. "Unfortunately, girls, I didn't see or hear anyone. But . . . I did smell something out of place."

"Smell?" Darcy repeated.

"What?" I asked, gripping the footboard of the bed. "What did you smell?"

"Perfume," he said. "Lots of it."

Chapter

10

Darcy and I waited until Psychic Nurse took a bathroom break. Then we snuck back out of the hospital and ran over to our bikes.

"Now we have proof that Zane didn't set the fire!" I said, exhilarated.

"He clearly doesn't wear perfume," Darcy agreed. "The arsonist is a girl!"

"We did it," I said in disbelief. "We saved him."

I was so happy and in the moment that, without thinking, I reached my fist out. And Darcy, equally thrilled with what we'd done, bumped it.

Then our smiles dropped as we realized we were supposed to be in a fight. We weren't supposed to be doing our special best-friend fist bump. I awkwardly looked down and started fiddling with my bike's kickstand.

"We should talk," Darcy said. "And not about cases. About us."

I nodded and let go of my bike. I didn't know what Darcy was going to say, and it felt like a butterfly sanctuary had set up in my stomach. We sat down beside each other on the curb.

Darcy began, "I was really mad at you. But now that we've been working the case together . . . I just can't stay mad. You're my best friend, you know. And, yeah, things might be changing a bit, but —"

"They're not changing," I protested.

"But . . . you joined the Dance Committee and you're hanging out with all these popular girls."

"The only popular girl I'm friends with is Fiona! And she's just as much friends with you. The only reason I joined the committee was as a favor to her and to be honest, I'd much rather be home reading my favorite astronomy blog. Or" — I paused to take a deep breath — "hanging out with you." I saw Darcy give a small smile, and I continued, "When we had our fight, you didn't really give me a chance to talk, and I think there were a few miscommunications."

"I guess I did interrupt you a lot," Darcy admitted. "What did you want to say?"

"About the day you invited me to come watch TV," I began.

Darcy piped up. "And you said you were too busy, but then you invited Fiona over and watched a movie with her instead."

I shook my head. "It wasn't like that. I was too busy to watch *Crime Scene: New York* with you. But as Fiona and I were leaving your house, she begged me to let her pick out my clothes for the next day. You know how into style she is and all that. So she came in, picked out my clothes, and then my parents invited her to stay for family movie night. And I didn't even think to call you because it was a movie you would've hated, I knew you were busy watching your favorite show, and I never thought you'd assume I was having secret hang-out time with Fiona. I thought you knew me better than that."

A little pink bloomed on Darcy's cheeks. "Oh."

Everything I'd been wanting to explain to my BFF spilled out in a rush. "And when I talked about having a sleepover and inviting Fiona and Maya, I never knew you were upset, because you faked being asleep.

All you had to say was, 'Norah, I was hoping we could hang out just the two of us,' and I totally would've done that."

"Oh," Darcy said again.

"There were lots of times when you took things I said the wrong way. But instead of asking me about it, you just kept it all bottled up inside until you exploded that day. It wasn't fair."

"You're right," she said. She looked down and started nervously playing with a pebble. "I just thought that you were beginning to . . . like Fiona better than me. Because she's popular and all that."

My eyes nearly bulged out of my head. "Since when do I care about who's popular and who's not?"

"I know you don't. But I just felt like you were . . . changing. You were hanging out with Fiona a lot and then you started dressing like her."

"Just that one day," I pointed out.

But then I remembered when I saw Darcy fist bump Hunter in the auditorium. And that bit of jealousy I had. That was how Darcy had felt when she'd seen me hanging with Fiona all the time.

"I'm really sorry," I said. My throat felt tight, like I was on the verge of crying. I fought to hold the tears back. "I'm not changing. I'm still nerdy old Norah and I always happily will be. I don't think there's anything wrong with making more friends, though. You like Fiona and Maya."

"I do. You're right," Darcy said. "And I'm sorry for acting the way I did. It all could've been avoided if I'd just told you how I was feeling."

"That's true," I said, finger raised high.

She held her fist out. "Friends?"

I bumped it. "Best friends. And partners in crime. Always."

She then reached across the space between us and pulled me in for a hug. Which was huge because Darcy is *not* a hugger. When we pulled away, there were even a few tears in her eyes. Tears! From Darcy! So then I started crying out of happiness. My best friend was back.

And I knew for a fact, deep down inside, the way you know that the sky is blue and the sun will set that night and rise the next day . . . that Darcy hadn't started the fire. No matter how mad she was at me, she would never want to hurt me or Zane.

———

Friday morning, I practically skipped into school. Darcy and I were finally and truly made up! I no longer felt like my insides were playing a game of Twister. And I was super excited to share what we'd found out with Principal Plati and get Zane off the hook.

But the school secretary told me the principal was at an offsite meeting with the superintendent and the earliest he could meet with me was after lunch. I took that appointment — I had no choice, really — and wished for time to go faster.

In math class, I finished my quiz early and used the rest of the time to sit and fantasize about my upcoming hero moment. I'd go to Zane's house and knock on his door. He'd open it, his face all depressed, and I'd tell him the good news. His eyes would brighten. He'd lift me up and spin me around in the air. And then he'd ask me to the dance and everything would be right with the world.

"Earth to Norah. Hellooooo? Are you here or out exploring the galaxy?"

I blinked quickly. Darcy was waving her hand in my face.

"Oh, sorry," I said. "I was just . . ."

"Daydreaming about telling Zane you saved him."

Yep, Darcy knew me better than anyone. Caught, I shrugged and smiled.

"Well class is over, dork," she said lovingly. "Time for lunch."

I bought a salad and a side of fries, grabbed extra ketchup, and then made my way through the lunch-room chaos to our usual corner table. Maya and Fiona were already seated. Darcy came over next, and I noticed Fiona eyeballing her outfit: black patterned tights under a purple-and-black-striped sweater dress. Pure Darcy.

Maya said brightly, "Hey, Norah, like my Delanceys?"

I furrowed my brow. "Your what?"

She stretched out her leg and flexed her foot. "My new Delancey shoes! Aren't they awesome?"

I took a peek. They were black leather ballet flats with a silver buckle on the front toe. Nicer looking than the sneakers I wore most days, but they didn't look as comfortable. Maya was totally excited, though, so I said, "Yeah, cool!"

Then I noticed Fiona wrinkling her nose in distaste. "What's up with you?" I asked.

Fiona put her hand to her collarbone. "I was the first one to wear Delancey flats. Then everyone else started buying them. It seemed like every girl on the Dance Committee had them on." She rolled her eyes at the fashion injustice.

Maya blushed. I gave her a sympathetic look and said, "Don't mind Miss Runway over here. You know how she gets with fashion. I think the shoes look great on you no matter who else has them."

"Sorry," Fiona said. "All I meant was that people should have their own style. I mean, look at Darcy. She may dress like a homeless vampire, but I have to admit she has her own creative look. Darcy, Violet, and I are the fashion visionaries at this school."

"Well, aren't you special?" I joked, tossing a French fry at Fiona's plate. Meanwhile, Darcy looked surprised at Fiona's compliment.

Fiona tossed the fry back, and we laughed and started a mini food fight until the lunch monitor told us to knock it off.

I was so glad everything was back to normal. Hanging out with my friends — and specifically Darcy again — had temporarily gotten my mind off the meeting with the principal. Though I didn't know why I was nervous about it. It was a *good* thing. Right?

The bell rang, and Darcy, Maya, and Fiona looked right at me.

It was time.

"Good luck," Maya said. She seemed anxious for me.

Darcy asked, "Are you sure you don't want me to go with you?"

Fiona scoffed. "Any meeting with the principal is better without Miss Troublemaker around."

"Touché," Darcy said, laughing. She'd been in the principal's office enough over the years. This was better for me to do myself.

I stood, ready. I was on my own, but armed with evidence. This whole nightmare was going to end. Now.

A few minutes later I sat in the chair outside the office. The longer I waited, the more my confidence melted into nervousness. I pulled the cuffs of my sweatshirt over my hands.

Finally, the secretary said, "Mr. Plati will see you now, Norah. Go on in."

I took a deep breath and walked into his office. Principal Plati looked up from a pile of folders on his desk. "Good afternoon, Norah. Have a seat."

He motioned to one of the chairs opposite his desk. I picked the left one and sat down.

"What can I help you with today?" he asked.

I clasped my sweaty hands together on my lap. "I'm here with evidence proving that Zane Munro didn't burn the field house down."

Mr. Plati's eyebrows rose halfway up his forehead. "Is that so? And what evidence is this?"

"Darcy and I visited Mr. Gray in the hospital yesterday afternoon," I began.

Mr. Plati held up his hand. "You did what?" he snapped.

I swallowed hard. "We just wanted to ask him if he'd seen or heard anything —"

"That is a job for the police, young lady," he cut in. "You have no place questioning people."

Part of me wanted to run away and hide under a desk somewhere. But I forged on. "Mr. Plati, I really believe Zane is innocent. Someone else set the fire and left his wallet there to frame him. And I felt that the only way to prove it was to talk with Mr. Gray. I'm sorry if you're upset about that, but I got the proof we needed. So I think it turned out okay."

Mr. Plati considered this for a moment, while banging the end of a pen against his desk. "Fine. Tell me what you found out."

Back on track, my heart slowed from the speed it had revved up to. I spoke clearly and confidently. "Mr. Gray said that when he went to try to put out the fire, in addition to smelling smoke, he noticed an overwhelming scent of perfume. And, sir, since Zane doesn't wear perfume, I think this rules him out as a suspect. I think we can assume the real arsonist is a girl."

Principal Plati groaned and rubbed his face with both hands, like I'd just made him overwhelmingly annoyed. "Is that it?" he said.

I wasn't expecting a standing ovation or anything, but his reaction was the complete opposite of what I had anticipated.

"Yes, that's it," I said, my tone a lot less confident. "Isn't that enough to prove it wasn't Zane?"

Mr. Plati pinched the bridge of his nose and inhaled deeply. "This is something the police haven't released to the media, and I shouldn't even be telling you. But you're a bright, well-behaved young lady, Norah. And I want you to stop this nonsense and focus on your schoolwork." He paused. "The fire department's investigation has shown that the fire started in a trash can pushed into the center of the field house. If the sprinkler system had been completely finished, it would've gone off and prevented the total destruction of the field house. But unfortunately the system wasn't turned on yet and the fire spread from the trash can and eventually engulfed the entire building."

"Okay . . ." I said, totally not understanding what this had to do with my evidence of Zane's innocence.

"The investigation also showed the initial cause of the fire. Someone piled napkins and dry grass inside the trash can, covered it with perfume, and lit it. The perfume was an accelerant. That's why Mr. Gray smelled what he did. The fire was *started* with perfume."

I felt a rumbling all through my body, like an

earthquake. Everything was crashing down. My evidence was not proof at all. Zane was still their main suspect. I wasn't about to head to Zane's house and tell him that I saved him.

So, instead, I ran into the hall in tears.

Chapter

11

Darcy was waiting for me in the hall.

"What happened?" she asked, grabbing my arm as she noticed my teary eyes.

"Why aren't you in class?" I asked back.

"I got a bathroom pass so I could wait out here for you. Who cares about that, what's wrong?"

I leaned up against a row of lockers. "Everything."

"Did you tell him about the perfume?" Darcy prodded.

I wiped my cheeks with the back of my hand. "Yeah. And he told me the fire had started with perfume. Someone poured it all over a bunch of napkins and stuff. That's why Mr. Gray smelled so much of it."

"Oh no," Darcy said, running her fingers through her hair.

I slid down the lockers until my butt hit the floor, and laid my face in my hands. "We've failed," I moaned. "We're never going to prove Zane's innocence. He's going to be charged. He's going to end up in juvie!"

"You're bugging out," Darcy said.

"I'm not bugging out."

"You are completely bugging out."

I looked up at her. "I know we were supposed to go see Mrs. Wolfson this afternoon and ask her about Charles Austin, but I just can't. I need to talk to Zane. I need to tell him that I failed."

Darcy reached down and pulled me back up to standing. "Look. His parents aren't even allowing him to talk to anyone. Plus, you don't need to say anything yet. We can still solve this case. Wait . . ." Her eyes flashed. "You're giving up!"

"I am not!" I said. And I wasn't. I totally wasn't. Okay, maybe a little bit. "But can you blame me?" I cried. "The odds are stacked against us."

Darcy tucked the purple strand of hair behind her ear. "News flash, Norah. We're twelve. We're geeks.

The odds are always stacked against us. But we always pull through. Together. And we will again."

"But what if this is the time that we don't?" I asked. I wasn't quitting, I was just being realistic.

"Meet me at your locker after the last bell. I'll think of something."

When the final bell sounded, all the other students ran out into the halls, bouncy and loud, barely able to contain their weekend excitement. But I shuffled along toward my locker like a mummy from a horror movie, my limbs hanging down, my head dipping low.

Until I saw Darcy, Fiona, and Maya waiting for me.

"What are you guys doing here?" I asked. I'd thought it would just be Darcy.

Maya stepped over to me and squeezed my shoulder. "Darcy told us the perfume lead didn't pan out."

Fiona flashed her brilliant smile. "So we all canceled our plans and we're going to spend the afternoon investigating together."

Fiona was probably the only one of us who had

plans, but I got what she was saying. They'd banded together to lift my spirits. To motivate me.

It was kind of working.

"One more thing." Darcy passed her cell phone to me. "You got a message."

Someone sent a text message to Darcy's phone for *me*? That didn't make any sense. I felt a twinge of nervousness, but Darcy had a huge smile. I looked down at the lit up screen.

norah, it's zane. i'm taking a chance 2 sneak out 1 message. i know u don't have a cell but i hope darcy will show this to u. thank u 4 believing in me. it means a lot. i miss u.

My heart flipped in my chest. Zane had risked his grounding to send me a secret message. He'd been thinking about me. He *missed* me. I knew I was blushing and grinning at the same time. The fog I'd been stuck in lifted, and I felt a jolt of determination.

"Let's do this," I said to the girls. "Any ideas?"

Darcy grinned — clearly, she knew Zane's text would encourage me. She said, "There's one place that we haven't checked for clues ... the crime scene."

"The field house?" I said, too loudly, and Maya shushed me. "Principal Plati said we were supposed to stay away from there," I whispered. "It's roped off."

Darcy shrugged. "We'll get as close as we can without going over the line."

Before we put our plan into action, I texted Zane back. My heart was pounding like crazy as I typed:

hi, it's norah. darcy and i are actually working on ur case. i miss u too.

That last part was the scariest to write, but I pressed SEND before I could chicken out. Then I passed the phone back to Darcy. I knew Zane probably wouldn't write back since his phone time was obviously limited. But I was so glad we'd been in touch.

Darcy, Fiona, Maya, and I took our time at our lockers and chatted outside for fifteen minutes. We weren't breaking any rules by going close to the field house, but we didn't want a crowd. After everyone had cleared out, we crept behind the school and crossed the grass, then the track, and finally got near the remains of the field house.

I could still smell the fire, even though it had long been put out. The charred building was surrounded by yellow police tape. As we got close, my hope started to fizzle. We couldn't go inside the building because it was unsafe, plus any clues would've been ashes by now. Even the area around the building was wrecked. The water from the giant fire hose had turned the dirt around the field house to mud.

"Any evidence that was here is gone now," I said.

"If only we'd looked closer that morning when we first got here," Maya said. "When the fire was still raging and we were all standing back, there might have been some clues left behind."

I heaved a breath. "We weren't looking for clues then. We were in shock and never figured the fire wasn't an accident."

Darcy was suspiciously quiet. She pulled her phone out of her pocket and turned it on.

"Expecting an important call?" Fiona joked.

But then I remembered. The morning of the fire, I saw Darcy walking around taking pictures with her phone.

"Did you get anything with those pictures you took?" I asked, hurrying to her side.

She started flipping through them. "I totally forgot I took them until just now. I mostly took photos of the fire itself because it looked cool. I wasn't thinking about evidence."

"Still," I said. "Maybe something's on there. Let's look."

We all crowded around as Darcy swiped each photo past. She was right, they were mainly pictures of the flames shooting out of the building. Until the last one.

"What's that?" Fiona asked.

"It was a mistake," Darcy said. "I meant to take another photo of the building but I ended up taking a picture of the ground."

I squinted at the photo, which was mostly brown. "Can you blow it up bigger?"

Darcy used two fingers on the screen to make the photo go close up. Her eyes widened as the photo did. "Holy guacamole! It's a footprint!"

Darcy handed the phone to me and I gasped. There was a distinct footprint in the dirt. "That wasn't made by a fireman's boot, either," I said. "It's small. Like a girl's shoe."

"And it's close to the building," Maya said. "None of the students were allowed that close."

"It's the arsonist's print," Darcy said, her eyes shining. "Made either when she entered or left the building!"

"Awesome!" Fiona said, grabbing the phone.

But I wasn't so sure this would help us. A footprint didn't tell us who the person was.

"I know what this is!" Fiona yelled.

We all stared at her.

"It's the Delancey flat!" she said.

"How could you know that?" I asked, astounded.

Fiona reached her hand out toward Maya. "Give me your shoe."

Maya frowned. "What?"

"You're wearing Delanceys, too," Fiona said quickly. "Just give me one."

Maya took off her right shoe and placed it in Fiona's hand. Fiona turned it over, exposing a design on the sole. "You know how Delancey shoes all have the same silver buckle on the toe? The designer put the imprint of the buckle on the sole, too."

"What for?" I asked.

"Her own special touch. A branding thing." Fiona

waved her hand as if that wasn't important. "Anyway, look at the dirt in the picture."

We all did, and understood. The design was there. Fiona was right. Whoever had set the fire had worn Delanceys.

And just like that, my mood lifted. It was like someone had taken a blanket off the sky and let the sun out. I had . . . hope.

We had a clue.

Chapter

The next morning, I went downstairs half asleep, following the scent of bacon. Dad had made breakfast, including his specialty: happy-face pancakes. I rubbed my eyes and dropped into a seat at the table.

"Morning, sleepyhead," Dad said, sliding a giant pancake on to my plate.

"Thanks," I answered, looking down at it. The pancake had chocolate chips for eyes, an orange slice for a mouth, and a piece of wavy bacon for hair. I cut into the chin area and took a bite.

I usually looked forward to weekends, but when I woke that morning I was actually sad that it was Saturday. Odd, I know, but I couldn't wait for the next school day so I could shoe-inspect every girl I saw.

The doorbell rang as Mom was setting the jug of orange juice on the table. Darcy was supposed to come over in a little bit, but she'd probably come early, lured by the scent of food like a wild animal.

"I'll get it," Dad called. A moment later he was back in the room with Darcy.

Mom smiled brightly. "Darcy, won't you join us for breakfast? There's plenty!"

Darcy slid into the seat across from me. "Thanks, Mrs. Burridge!"

Mom snuck me a little smile that said, *I'm so happy things are back to normal!* I knew she'd been worried about my argument with Darcy.

Mom poured Darcy a tall glass of OJ. "So what's new with you girls?" she asked. "You've been busy lately."

I finished chewing and said, "Yeah, I've had a lot of schoolwork. And I joined the Dance Committee with Fiona." *And we're trying to solve two cases.*

"The Dance Committee?" Mom said, looking pleasantly surprised. "You're really expanding your horizons."

I shrugged. "I don't even know if I'll be going to the dance."

Darcy froze with her fork in midair. "Why not?"

"You know why," I hissed. I didn't want to get into the whole Zane thing in front of my parents. It was awkward enough to discuss crushes without bringing up the fact that the boy you liked was a suspected criminal.

"But even if . . ." Darcy struggled to disguise her words. "If . . . that *thing* doesn't work out, you can still go without a date."

"Thing?" Mom asked.

"What date?" Dad asked, looking alarmed.

I clumsily dropped my fork, and it clanged loudly against the plate. "Um, there's no thing. No date. There's just this . . . dance," I stammered out quickly. "And — and I was hoping that a boy I liked would be there. But it looks like he's not going." I stared at my plate and wondered if it was possible to die from embarrassment. "Can we not talk about this anymore?" I asked.

Mom and Dad shared one of their parent looks. "Sure," Mom began. "But if you ever do want to talk about it —"

"I know, Mom!" I said, in a forced happy tone. "Thanks!"

After breakfast, Darcy and I hopped on our bikes and finally headed toward Mrs. Wolfson's house. There was nothing we could do on Zane's case until Monday. So our plans for the weekend were to research the Prom Killer.

Sheesh, that sounds weird. One of these weekends I'm going to just stay home and bake cupcakes, I swear.

If Mrs. Wolfson had gone to high school with Charles Austin, maybe she could shed some light on what happened that infamous night. It was worth a try.

We laid our bikes on the grass and walked up the freshly painted porch steps to Mrs. Wolfson's door. Darcy knocked, and we stood patiently waiting for Mrs. Wolfson. She walked with a cane so it took her a little longer to get around. After a minute or so, I saw the telltale flutter of the window curtains and then the door swung open.

"Girls!" Mrs. Wolfson called. "I'm so happy you're here! Come in, come in. I baked some fudge brownies you've just got to try."

"Yes!" Darcy said, doing a little shimmy as she walked through the doorway.

Darcy and I made ourselves comfortable on the big flowered couch in the living room while Mrs. Wolfson served us brownies on fancy china and milk in teacups. I was still full from breakfast, but took a bite to be polite. And, wow, that was a fantastic brownie. I suddenly wasn't too full after all.

"I'm so glad you stopped by," Mrs. Wolfson said. She tucked a loose strand of her long gray hair back into the bun on top of her head. "The house looks so beautiful. I wanted to thank you again for getting all your friends to help out."

My heart felt all warm and proud. "It was no problem."

Darcy, always one to get right to the point, said, "So, Mrs. Wolfson. We were checking out old school yearbooks and saw that you graduated from high school here in Danville."

"Oh, yes, I sure did," she said, nodding. "My high school is actually your girls' middle school now."

"We know," I said. "We were doing some reading about . . ." My voice trailed off as I tried to find the most sensitive way to bring the topic up.

"Your prom night," Darcy finished for me. "The fire. Were you there?"

The teacup paused halfway to Mrs. Wolfson's mouth and her eyes got a faraway look to them. "Yes," she said softly. "It was supposed to be the most magical night of our lives. Instead . . . it was terrible."

"What do you remember?" Darcy said, leaning so far forward I thought she was going to fall off the couch.

Mrs. Wolfson laid her cup down on the saucer. "It started out beautifully. The music, the decorations. But then came the smell, the smoke . . . and the screams."

I shuddered at the thought. "Did you know the boy who died? Charles Austin?"

The corner of her mouth lifted up in a tiny smile. "Everyone knew Charlie. He was the most well-liked boy in our school."

I set my teacup down on the table and noticed my hand shaking a bit. That night had just been a story in the newspaper, a legend, something that happened long ago. It wasn't until I sat here with Mrs. Wolfson, listening to her speak, that I fully realized it was something true. Charlie had been a real person. Sadness seeped through me.

Darcy said, "The article we read said that Charles wouldn't leave the building because he was looking for 'his girl' but his date was already outside. Why the confusion?"

"Because his date wasn't his girl," Mrs. Wolfson answered matter-of-factly.

Darcy and I looked at each other.

"There was another girl?" I asked, confused.

Mrs. Wolfson looked off into the distance. Her voice took on a dreamlike quality. "Charles Austin and Helen Fallon were friends for a long time. Everyone knew that Helen loved Charles, and we were starting to think that Charlie loved her back. There were rumors that they were going to prom together. But then Betty Frazier asked Charlie to prom."

She said that last part dramatically, but I didn't get it. "Okay . . ." I said.

"I know in this day and age, it's not a big deal for a girl to ask a boy out," Mrs. Wolfson explained, "but back then it was very forward of Betty. Though Betty and Charlie did make sense. Betty was the prettiest, most popular girl. What boy would turn her down?"

"So he went to the prom with Betty and not Helen?" I asked, trying to keep it straight in my mind.

"Yes. Helen was so distraught that she didn't go with anyone. She stayed home alone. Though, Charlie wouldn't leave the building because he swore he saw her there."

"And *was* she there?" Darcy chimed in.

Mrs. Wolfson gave us a skeptical look. "No. She never went to the dance. People think that the fire messed with Charlie's mind. Maybe he felt guilty about dropping Helen for Betty and he thought he saw her in the smoke." She paused to take a sip of tea. "In any case, we'll never know what he saw. He perished in the flames."

A chill ran across my skin. "Do you know what happened to Betty and Helen?"

"Betty married some handsome young man and moved to the West Coast. Helen never married. Sometimes I wonder if it's because she never got over Charlie. She's still here in town."

Darcy straightened. "Do you know where?"

"Yes. At the Maples Nursing Home," Mrs. Wolfson said.

Darcy looked at me, eyes aflame. I knew that look. Helen Fallon was going to get a visit soon. From us.

On Sunday, we tried to visit Helen at the nursing home, but were told by the woman at the front desk that Helen wasn't feeling well and couldn't accept visitors. We'd have to try again in a few days.

On Monday morning at school, I walked the hallway with my head down, eyes peeled for the Delancey-wearing arsonist.

But by the time I reached my locker I'd already seen two girls wearing the shoes. I opened a notebook and jotted down their names, but a pit was beginning to form in my stomach. What if too many girls wore that brand? I sighed. Why did the arsonist have to be so trendy?

Darcy strolled up to my locker with a notebook in hand and a pencil behind her ear. "I've been patrolling the hallways, and I've got four shoe suspects already!"

That pit I mentioned before? Yeah, it was growing.

"You say that like it's a good thing," I mumbled.

Frowning, Darcy said, "This *was* the plan, right?"

I shrugged. "Yeah, but I figured maybe like three girls would have the shoes. Then we could rule out those with alibis, figure out who was here early the day of the fire, and bam. Arsonist exposed. But we already have six names before first period! This clue isn't going to help us much at all."

I gazed down at the floor as yet another pair of Delanceys approached.

"Did you guys see the posters?" Maya asked nervously.

I looked up into her worried brown eyes. "What posters?"

"We've been focused downward this morning," Darcy explained, motioning at Maya's shoes.

Maya suddenly looked uncomfortable. I wondered how she felt about owning the same shoes the arsonist wore. I noticed Darcy giving Maya a long stare, and I knew the gears were grinding in her head. But I wouldn't suspect Maya. No way. She was friends with Zane. She wouldn't frame him.

Maya tugged on my shirtsleeve and said, "Come with me."

Darcy and I followed her around the corner. Even though it was hopeless, I continued to scan shoes along the way. Until I nearly walked into Violet and Amanda, only one of which was wearing Delanceys.

Before I could figure out who was who and why they would stop and stand in the middle of the busiest hallway, Darcy squeezed my hand and pointed up.

The big dance banner hung on the wall, but it looked a bit different this morning. It had been vandalized.

More people came to stop and stare. Their whispers filled the hallway.

"*Who would write that?*"

"*This is creepy.*"

"*I don't even want to go anymore.*"

I ignored the comments as my eyes traveled over the words that had been painted across the banner. Words that felt like a threat.

THE PROM KILLER IS BACK.

Chapter

13

Clearly the Prom Killer was not stalking the halls of Danville Middle School. Whoever set that fire was either dead or eighty years old now. And why would they want to stir up trouble again, after all this time? Our fire had nothing to do with the Prom Killer. My logical mind knew this.

The rest of the school? Not so much.

Kids went bananas. Some were convinced that a ghost was haunting the halls. Some were even saying they were too scared to go to the dance. Rumors flew that the field house was only the first fire. The Prom Killer was going to return on the night of the dance and burn down the gym with everyone in it.

By the end of the day, even Fiona was in a tizzy. She ran up to my locker, basically panting in panic. "There's a rumor that Principal Plati might cancel the dance!"

I twirled my combination on the dial and opened the locker door. "Because someone wrote something stupid on a poster?" I scoffed. I hardly believed that.

Fiona stomped her foot. "Because people are freaking out and therefore their parents will freak out. Zane hasn't been arrested yet. He's still just a suspect. So people are starting to wonder if the Prom Killer story is coming true again. If history will repeat itself."

I felt a flicker of doubt. "They wouldn't cancel the dance altogether, though. Right?"

"Yeah, they would," Darcy said, coming up behind me. She hefted her backpack up over one shoulder. "They take this stuff seriously. If there's even a small chance the dance is unsafe, it will be canceled for sure."

I could feel the blood draining from my face. Only a few days ago, everything had been wonderful. Zane was about to ask me to the dance. Then Zane was framed. We didn't solve the case. And now the dance might be canceled.

My throat tightened as a mixture of anger and sadness rushed through me. "It's just so unfair. All of this."

"I know!" Fiona agreed, raising her fist in the air. "The Dance Committee worked so hard. We're having our last meeting Wednesday afternoon to make decorations. Saturday night is going to be perfect. Unless it gets canceled."

"It won't if we solve the case first," Darcy said, trying to remain hopeful.

But I wasn't so sure.

Tuesday afternoon, Darcy and I decided to try and visit the Maples Nursing Home again.

The same woman was behind the desk. She had a big pouf of hair that she'd probably meant to dye red but looked kind of pink. She remembered us. "Here to see Helen?" she asked.

"Yes," I answered. "If she's well."

The woman made a face that worried me. "As well as she's going to get, I'm afraid. Go on down the hall. She's in the first room on your right."

"That was kind of ominous," Darcy whispered as we walked.

We found Helen's room quickly enough. It was large and homey looking, with a bright and big window, a bed, a television set, a small couch, and a rocking chair. A thin, frail-looking woman rocked in the chair while staring out the window.

Darcy coughed into her hand. "Excuse me? Are you Helen Fallon?"

The woman slowly turned her head toward us. She wore a flowered housedress and had short, thinning white hair. "Yes, I am," she said, glancing from Darcy to me in confusion.

I gingerly approached the chair, suddenly nervous. She was just a little old lady, nothing to be scared of, but something about her seemed ghostlike and sad. "We'd like to talk to you for a few minutes, if that's all right."

"About what?" she asked warily.

I opened my mouth to speak, but the words didn't come.

Darcy had no such problem. "About prom night, 1948."

The woman's eyes widened. After a long pause, she motioned to the couch opposite her chair. "Have a seat."

Darcy and I settled in on the couch, and Helen turned toward us. She was too skinny and seemed sickly. She let out a bone-shaking cough into her fist.

I looked at Darcy and grimaced. That must have been what the woman behind the desk meant. Helen was dying. I felt guilty interrogating her about something that had happened so long ago. We should let her sit in peace. Yet, at the same time, she'd invited us to stay. Maybe she *wanted* to talk about it.

"So," Helen said. "What do you want to know?"

I nudged Darcy with my elbow. She could start.

Darcy cleared her throat. "Um, I don't know if you heard, but our field house burned down. At your old school."

Helen nodded. "Unfortunate. I read about that in the paper."

"We were supposed to have our dance in that building," Darcy explained. "So, our fire has brought up stories about . . ."

"My fire," Helen said matter-of-factly.

"Yes," I chimed in. "Rumors and ghost stories. We know that you and the boy who died were close, and I feel bad even asking you these questions, but we were hoping —"

Helen put her hand up. She held me in a steely gaze, like she was making some momentous decision. After what seemed like forever, she simply said, "It's time."

"Time for what?" I asked. Time for us to leave?

"It's time for the truth," she said, and her voice didn't sound frail anymore. It had force behind it. She sat up a bit straighter in her seat and said, "I've kept it in for so long. A lifetime really. It's time for my story to be told."

I could feel Darcy trembling with anticipation beside me. "Okay . . ." she said.

Helen clasped her hands on her lap and met our eyes. "I set the fire."

I stared at her in shock. "What?"

"Prom. Nineteen forty-eight. I set the fire," she repeated.

Darcy and I sat in stunned silence. If I were the fainting type, I would have dropped to the floor.

"I loved Charlie Austin," Helen began. "And I do believe he was starting to return my feelings. Even though he was much more popular than I was, he'd asked me to prom. It was a dream come true."

Helen beamed at the memory. Then the smile slipped from her face as she said, "But then Betty Frazier and her boyfriend suddenly broke up. She was beautiful, a stunner really. And she decided she wanted Charlie by her side at the prom."

"What did he do?" Darcy asked.

"He dropped me. Just like that. The day before prom. I was dateless and heartbroken. Embarrassed and ashamed."

My heart sank, imagining how Helen must have felt. But then I remembered . . . she wasn't so innocent after all. I said, "But you went to prom night anyway."

Helen took a deep breath. "I didn't want anyone to get hurt, you should know that. All I wanted was to spoil the prom. Since it had already been ruined for me. I set a small fire in a darkened corner. I figured it would start slowly, they'd all run out, and the dance would end early. But the decorations caught and the flames spread too quickly."

I shuddered, picturing the moment. My fingers crept toward Darcy until they found her hand to clasp on to. Hers felt as clammy as mine.

Helen's eyes were wild and the words started to come faster. "There was panic and horror. Everyone made it out but Charlie . . . he spotted me. I ran out the back door. He went out front and didn't see me in the crowd. So he went back in and refused to come out until he'd found me. He felt guilty, I think. But he didn't realize I'd left the building . . . and he died in there."

I clutched my stomach, feeling sick. Darcy looked even paler than usual.

Helen continued, "When he was still in the building searching for me, I was halfway down the street, running home, gripped with guilt over what I'd done. And I was only feeling terrible about the fire. I didn't find out anyone was hurt until the next morning. Charlie was dead, and it was my fault."

Helen's bloodshot eyes were wet and glassy. Her voice broke. "I never got over it. I never allowed myself to date or marry or have children because Charlie would never have those things." Her voice cracked, and she let out a rattling cough.

I recoiled deeper into the couch. I wished I could click my heels three times and be back at home, without these scary images in my head. But Darcy squeezed my hand, silently telling me to be brave.

After she regained her composure, Helen said, "His death was accidental. But that doesn't make it any less my fault." Tears slicked her face as she focused her gaze on us. "You can do what you wish with this information. Go to the police. Whatever you feel you have to do. But learn this lesson from me, girls. Love can be the most wonderful thing. But jealousy will bring about your darkest hour."

Helen launched into another coughing fit. She turned her back to us and resumed gazing out the window, perhaps thinking about her crime. Darcy and I exchanged a glance and managed to walk numbly out of her room. We didn't speak a word as we got to our bikes, still dazed.

Darcy broke the silence. "Well, that was unexpected."

I nodded. When I'd entered Helen's room, I never for a moment guessed that she would be the infamous Prom Killer. I swallowed hard. "What should we do? She's guilty of something horrible."

Darcy shook her head. "I know. But she never meant to harm anyone."

Thinking out loud, I said, "Yeah, but doesn't she need to be punished?"

"She punished *herself* for her entire life," Darcy said. "Plus, you saw her. She's not going to live much longer."

That was true. What did I want . . . for her to spend the last week of her life in jail? "The whole thing is just so sad," I said. "The tragedy could've been prevented to begin with. But once it happened, Helen should've been brave and told the truth right away."

"I agree," Darcy said. "But it's in our hands now. So what do we do about it?"

I took a deep breath and thought about everything we'd learned. "I think what Helen and Charles would want is for people to learn from the mistakes *they* made, and to not repeat them."

Darcy nodded. "When this is all over, we'll talk to Mrs. Wolfson. She'll help us figure out the right thing to do."

Chapter

14

Wednesday, I still felt rattled from our discovery of the real Prom Killer. But in addition to all these mixed-up feelings about 1948, I also felt heartened. We'd done it. We followed the clues right to the real Prom Killer. I felt a flicker of hope that we'd be able to do the same for our very own fire starter.

When I got to the Dance Committee meeting, I could hear squeals of excitement from the girls inside. I walked in just as Fiona was banging her gavel on the podium to start the meeting.

Violet rolled her eyes at the sight of me.

"Word has come from Principal Plati that the dance will *not* be canceled," Fiona said. "So it's time for decorations!"

The crowd clapped and cheered. Fiona took charge, breaking everyone into stations. I was assigned to glitter duty, which was perfect. My job was to go from table to table, tossing my glitter on any decoration that needed it. So I could move around the room, listen to conversations, and keep my eyes open for clues.

Fiona instructed everyone to spread out their supplies. People had been put in charge of bringing paper, glue, scissors, and other stuff. I wandered around with my tub of glitter, stopping to sprinkle it on stars here and there. A few girls wore Delanceys, but — since most girls don't wear the same shoes every day — some who wore them yesterday weren't wearing them today. Which made it even more confusing.

By the time the meeting was finishing up, the room was a disaster area. Backpacks, papers, and remnants of cutouts were strewn about everywhere. I stayed behind with a few others to help clean up.

Mrs. Haymon, the teacher-advisor, held up the recycling bin as I dumped a bunch of cut-up paper into it. "Thanks for helping, Norah," she said.

Even though I wasn't feeling very cheery, I gave Mrs. Haymon a smile and said, "No problem." She was one of my favorite teachers. Her mind was a lot like mine — focused on logic and reason — and we'd had a couple cool talks about astronomy in the past.

I bent down to pick a pile of trash off the floor, when I saw something that made my heart lodge in my throat.

It was a piece of notebook paper that must have fallen out of someone's book or backpack during a supply rummage. It was only a girly doodle of a heart with a boy's name in the middle. Nothing earth-shattering.

Except the name was Zane.

And the nice happy heart had a giant, dark X crossed over it.

Apparently, I wasn't the only one on the Dance Committee with Zane on the brain. But this person seemed to have . . . conflicted emotions about him.

I looked around the room. There was no way to tell who it came from. Half the committee members had already left. But as I looked down at the note again, something in the back of my mind tingled. I squinted and stared until I realized what was nagging at me.

I'd seen this handwriting before.

"Someone else on the Dance Committee likes Zane," I said, handing Darcy the note. I'd hurried to her house with my heart racing and we were now in her basement. "Well, *liked* is probably the more appropriate word. Now they seem to hate him."

Darcy examined the note for a minute, deep in thought. Then she looked up at me. "The field house fire ties in to the Prom Killer after all."

I gulped. "Say what?"

She dropped the note on the couch and started pacing. "This whole time we've been thinking, 'Why would anyone do this? Everyone likes Zane.'"

I shrugged. "Yeah, so?"

She opened her arms wide. "Maybe that's it then. Someone *likes* Zane. Maybe someone jealous enough to want to ruin his life because he likes . . . someone else instead." She made googly eyes at me rather than saying my name.

I blushed, but then thought for a moment. "Helen was so jealous over Charlie taking Betty to the prom that she set out to ruin their night." I pointed to the note. "And this person found out that Zane was going to ask me to the dance and decided if she couldn't go with him, no one could?"

Darcy nodded and rubbed her chin. "That would make sense. How would this other girl find that out, though?"

I had a theory. "Can I borrow your cell phone for a minute?"

Darcy pulled it out of her pocket and handed it over. I scrolled down to Fiona's number and hit CALL. After two rings, Fiona picked up. "Hello?"

"Hey, it's Norah. I'm using Darcy's phone."

I could hear the smack of bubble gum. "What's up?" she asked between chews.

"Did you tell anyone anything about Zane and me?"

The chewing stopped. "Like what?"

"That he might like me or something like that."

The line was silent for a moment. Then Fiona said, "Promise you won't get mad?"

I sighed. "I promise."

"I may have said that you and Zane were totally crushing on each other and that he was definitely going to ask you to the dance."

I smacked my face into my palm.

"I'm sorry!" Fiona said. "But you know how I am with gossip. It's like a compulsion. I can't *not* talk about these things with people."

"Fine, fine." I wasn't too mad. She was about to give us our biggest clue. "Okay, Fiona, this is very important. You need to remember. Who did you tell?"

"Um, it was at the Dance Committee meeting the week before the fire."

"Okay . . ." I said. "And *who* did you tell?"

A pause. "Everyone at the meeting."

After a lot of groaning on my end and apologizing on her end, I got off the phone and filled Darcy in. She rolled her eyes about Fiona's big mouth, but said, "That could be the arsonist's motive, though."

Helen's words echoed in my head. *Jealousy will bring about your darkest hour.* Was someone really jealous enough — of Zane and *me* — to commit a crime?

"So how do we figure out who it is?" I blurted.

"We need a Partners in Crime brainstorm," Darcy replied. "Hang on."

She went into the corner and dragged a big white-board on an easel into the center of the room. She uncapped one marker and handed me another.

"Where did this come from?" I asked.

"Found it at a yard sale," she said. "I knew it would come in handy. Detectives use these all the time on crime shows. It helps to write down all the clues and then you can see patterns you didn't realize were there."

I was willing to try anything. "Okay, where do we begin?"

She spoke out loud as she wrote. "The arsonist is a girl, and she's on the Dance Committee."

The marker squeaked as she scribbled.

<u>CLUES</u>

GIRL

DANCE COMMITTEE

"She wears Delanceys," I said.

Darcy wrote: DELANCEY SHOES.

"What else do we have?" she asked.

I looked at the note in my hand and remembered my realization from the meeting. "The handwriting is big, round, and looping. And notice the tiny heart doodled inside the *e* on *Zane*."

"Great!" Darcy said. "Distinctive handwriting!"

"There's more," I said. "I first noticed this strange *e* on the dance posters that were hung in school . . . the morning of the fire."

Darcy's eyes gleamed. "So whoever wrote this note also put up the first posters."

"Yep," I said. "And whoever did it came into school extra early on that day to hang them. But when Fiona asked at the Dance Committee who did it . . . no one raised their hand."

"Because that would place her at school early the morning of the fire," Darcy said, marker raised in the air. She turned to the board and wrote: HUNG THE DANCE POSTERS.

Then she started a second column and wrote:
TIMELINE
STARTED FIRE
HUNG POSTERS
E-MAILED ZANE FROM COMPUTER LAB

"It looks like she came in early to start the fire," I said, "but she needed an alibi in case she got caught on school grounds."

"So she hung the posters in case anyone saw her around," Darcy said. "And then she had extra time to e-mail Zane from the computer lab while everyone else was gathering outside."

"Exactly." I tapped a fingernail on the board. "Now for suspects."

I made a third column with the word <u>SUSPECTS</u>.

"You know who's on Dance Committee and has the right shoes?" Darcy said with one eyebrow raised.

I shook my head. "Don't say Maya."

"Maya!" Darcy cried.

I glared at her.

"What?" Darcy made a face. "She's a legit suspect. She and Zane have gotten close, being neighbors and all."

"She's also neighbors with Hunter," I pointed out. "Maybe she has a crush on him, too?"

Something flashed in Darcy's eyes. But as quickly as it came, it disappeared. "Hunter's not the one in trouble right now," she said.

I gave an annoyed sigh. "Maya was excited to tell me Zane's secret was that he liked me. She wasn't jealous."

"Fine, then," Darcy said reluctantly. "Is there anyone on Dance Committee who *does* act jealous?"

Violet's sneer immediately came to mind.

Darcy pointed at my face. "You're thinking of someone. Who?"

"Well, Violet clearly has a problem with me. But I

assumed it was because my dance theme got chosen over hers."

Darcy narrowed her eyes. "That could be it. She *is* a girl who likes to get her way. But her anger about the theme could also be covering up her true jealousy . . . over Zane."

I stepped back and looked at our work on the board. It was frustrating to be so close yet still so far. "We have it," I said, clenching my fist. "We know everything this girl did and when she did it. We just don't know for sure *who* she is."

Darcy paced back and forth in front of the board, then suddenly stopped. She picked the note back up from the couch and tapped her finger on the unique *e*.

A slow smile spread on her face. "We don't know who she is, but we know how to catch her."

Chapter

15

Fiona stood waiting outside the classroom Thursday after the last bell.

"Thanks for calling an emergency meeting of the Dance Committee," I said breathlessly as I ran up to her. The day had flown by as I made sure every part of our plan was in place.

We were going to catch the arsonist. Now.

Assuming everyone did their part. This was a group effort.

"Is everyone coming?" I asked.

Fiona nodded quickly. "I pretended to be in full-blown panic mode and made sure everyone knew they had to come. Or else."

No one wanted an "or else" from Fiona. I was confi-dent of that.

Members started streaming in, so we had to stop chatting. "You know what to do?" I whispered.

"Just leave it to me," Fiona said. "This will be my crowning achievement in seventh-grade acting."

And with that, Fiona charged into the room and waited at the podium. I took the seat closest to the door. Mrs. Haymon was sitting in her usual seat, but she had no papers with her to grade. Just an empty desk. She gave me a single nod and I returned it.

When the room was full, Fiona banged her gavel.

"What's going on?" Violet snapped. "I thought we finished all the decorations yesterday."

Fiona waved her hand dismissively. "If we want the dance to be okay, then, yes, we finished. But I want nothing less than spectacular, and I'm sure the rest of you agree." She eyeballed the crowd until every girl nodded in agreement.

"Wonderful," she said. "Moving on. The first thing we need to create today requires beautiful hand-writing. So I would like everyone to come up to the board. You should all write one word, the same word, so we can compare and select the person whose hand-writing has the . . . flourish that I'm looking for. The word shall be" — Fiona cast a quick look and a wry smile at me — "*dance*."

I heard a few disgruntled mutters, but everyone lined up and took their turn at the board. Maya was first, wearing her Delanceys as usual. My stomach clenched, waiting for her to finish. She stepped away and I examined her *dance*.

No heart in the *e*. I let out the breath I'd been holding in.

Several girls started writing at the same time. I stared at their shoes and their handwriting in equal measure. No fancy *e* from any of them.

Last came Violet and Amanda. They walked to the whiteboard together, as they did almost everything else, selected markers, and started writing. When they finished and stepped back from the board, Fiona's eyes darted to mine.

My hand gripped my stomach, and I had to force myself not to audibly gasp.

The fancy *e* was on the board, with the little heart drawn inside.

We'd found her. I knew who had set the fire. I only hoped my secret weapon would come through.

Mrs. Haymon stood and said, "Meeting adjourned."

"What's going on?" someone whispered.

"What about the new decorations?"

"We're finished here," Mrs. Haymon said. "You can all go home. Except for you and you." She pointed at me and one other girl. "You're coming with me to the principal's office."

My legs were trembling as I followed Mrs. Haymon down the hall with the girl who'd set fire to the field house. There were so many things I wanted to say and ask, but I kept my eyes straight ahead. I had to be patient.

My mind whirred, putting it all together. I almost couldn't believe it. I'd suspected Violet, but it was actually her best friend. Amanda never stuck out to me as guilty because she'd been so . . . nice.

But the evidence was all there. Amanda was on the Dance Committee. And unlike Violet, who Fiona said had her own sense of style, Amanda wore

Delanceys. And she put a happy little heart inside of her lowercase *e*'s.

Now that I knew, little things were making more sense. Like that time Amanda and I spoke in the hallway and she'd said she was sure Zane "didn't mean for any of this to happen." It had seemed like an innocent comment at the time. Now it had much more meaning. *Amanda* clearly hadn't meant for the fire to get so out of control. Well, it was too late now.

We reached the office waiting area and there sat Darcy, her knee nervously bobbing up and down. Her eyes widened as she saw Amanda with me. She hadn't been totally sure that we'd find the culprit. But the plan had worked, thanks to Mrs. Haymon.

I had met with her early in the morning and explained our predicament. As a math teacher, Mrs. Haymon appreciated logic and reasoning. So I'd laid everything out for her. We knew Zane had been framed because of the e-mail, and I could attest to the fact that his wallet had been missing before the fire. We had motive from the note and crime scene evidence with the footprint. All we had to do was use the process of elimination to match the handwriting and we had our arsonist.

To be doubly sure, I told Mrs. Haymon that she could check the computer lab records. Though Darcy and I couldn't access them, Mrs. Haymon could. To use one of the computers, you have to log in with your school user name and password. Mrs. Haymon could check to see who logged in during the early morning hours the day of the fire. And if that person also had the telltale handwriting at the meeting, then we'd know for sure. I also explained how I'd already been to Mr. Plati once to plead Zane's case. It would mean a lot more coming from Mrs. Haymon.

Mrs. Haymon had agreed to look into the records and speak with Mr. Plati. And — if the handwriting showed up on the board during the meeting — we'd take it from there.

So now our entire case rested on what happened in the next five minutes.

We walked with Mrs. Haymon and Amanda into Mr. Plati's office, and we all took seats across from his desk. I had no idea what was going to happen next. I just hoped it didn't all backfire.

Mr. Plati clasped his hands on his desk. "Amanda, do you know why you've been called into my office?"

"No, sir," she said, though her voice was trembling.

"There isn't . . . anything you'd like to tell me?" he said, giving her one last chance to come clean.

I closed my eyes and hoped that she'd confess. *Do it*, I silently said. *Confess and this will all be over.*

"No," Amanda said. "Nothing."

My heart sank.

Mr. Plati stood and crossed his arms. He always looked more intimidating when he did that. Even *I* was scared, and I hadn't done anything wrong.

"We have a problem then, Amanda," he said firmly. "Did you know that I have security cameras in and around the school?"

"N-no," she nervously replied.

"And we just got finished going through the footage for the morning of the field house fire. And we were able to narrow down who was here early. I saw you, on video, hanging posters."

She nodded. "F-for the d-dance."

"Right." Mr. Plati lowered his voice a couple octaves. "I saw something else on the footage, too. It would be much easier on everyone involved if you'd admit it yourself before I have to say it. Would you like one last opportunity to do that, Amanda?"

She looked over at Darcy and me, and the guilt was written all over her face. She blinked her suddenly wet eyes and turned back toward Mr. Plati. In the smallest voice, she said, "It was me. I burned the field house down."

My mouth went dry. Hearing the words come out of Amanda made it real.

"Why?" Mr. Plati asked.

With a trembling hand, Amanda tugged her hair behind her ear. She cast a sidelong glance at me, her face bright red. "I heard Fiona talking about how Zane Munro liked Norah and that he was going to ask her to the dance. And I was just so mad."

"Because *you* like him," Darcy said.

"Yeah," she snapped. "And I couldn't believe he liked Norah the Nerd over me."

Since she was in the middle of a confession and all, I decided to let that one go.

She continued, "On that Friday, his wallet fell out of his pocket in class. I picked it up and — for some reason — I kept it. Then, Monday morning when I came in early to hang the posters . . . I started the fire and dropped his wallet so he'd be blamed. That way he couldn't go to the dance with Norah."

"But the entire field house burned to the ground," Mr. Plati said angrily.

"I didn't mean for that to happen." She sniffled. "I set a small fire in a trash can, with napkins and perfume. I never expected the fire to go past the trash can. I thought the sprinklers on the ceiling would go off and put it out. So, no real damage done, but Zane would get in trouble."

"But the sprinkler system wasn't finished yet," Mr. Plati said. "It wasn't on."

"I didn't know that," Amanda pleaded. "I didn't want to ruin the building. And I never wanted Mr. Gray to get hurt. Never in a million years. I didn't even want Zane to be in deep trouble. Just enough that he couldn't go to the dance."

"You should've told the truth right away," Mr. Plati said. "Because now you're the one in deep trouble."

Mr. Plati asked Mrs. Haymon, Darcy, and me to step outside while he called Amanda's parents. Mrs. Haymon had to go, but Darcy and I thanked her profusely for her help, and she thanked us for being so persistent in our research.

166

As Darcy and I stood in the hall, I couldn't believe it had all come together. Zane's suspension was over, but Amanda was about to get a new one — big time.

A few minutes later, Mr. Plati came out of his office and closed the door behind him.

"Amanda's parents will be coming now," he said. "You girls can go on your way. I'll take it from here."

That was good enough for me, but Darcy didn't budge.

"Wait a second." She tilted her head to the side and stared at the principal. "Mr. Plati, if you had the crime on video, why did you wait this long to bring that up?"

His lips tightened, fighting a smile. He whispered, "I *don't* have the crime on video."

Darcy gasped. "You bluffed?"

He laughed and turned back toward his office, saying over his shoulder, "What, you think you're the only ones in this school who can play detective?"

Chapter 16

Thursday night, the phone rang. I grabbed the cordless and ran into my room.

"Hello?" I said breathlessly.

"Norah? It's Zane!"

I hadn't heard his voice in over a week. And he sounded so happy. I thought my heart would burst. I nervously paced the room while I talked.

"I'm so glad you called," I said. "Have you been taken off suspension?"

"Yes! And my permanent record was cleared. Principal Plati even personally apologized. And it's all because of you."

I felt a blush spread from my neck to my forehead. "I had help," I said.

"Still. You never gave up." He grew quiet, and the silence stretched on for a long moment. "Norah?"

I stopped pacing and stood perfectly still. "Yes?"

"There's something I've wanted to ask you for a while."

I had to remind myself to breathe. "Okay . . ."

"Will, um . . . will you go to the dance with me?"

I flopped backward onto the bed and kicked my feet in the air. I tried to keep my voice cool and answered, "Yes, I will!"

I didn't even squeal or scream.

Until I hung up the phone.

I spent Saturday at the gym, blowing up balloons and hanging decorations with Maya, Fiona, and the rest of the Dance Committee. Well, everyone except Amanda, who'd been suspended and might end up expelled. We didn't know what the police were going to do, but rumor had it her parents made her apologize to Mr. Gray and grounded her to the age of, like, forty. While we decorated, it was all anyone talked about. Even Violet was shocked by her friend's crazy behavior.

After finishing up at the gym, I went home, showered, and started to get ready. Darcy came over, and we blasted music and sang into hairbrush microphones. "What do you think?" Darcy asked once she was ready. She gave a twirl. Her dress was black with a purple ribbon around the waist. And she wore her big black boots, of course.

"It's perfectly Darcy," I said, smiling.

I held my hands out and did a twirl of my own. I'd gone last-minute shopping at the mall with Fiona the night before and picked up a new dress and matching flats. The dress was silver with sparkling sequins on the bodice and a layered skirt that came to my knees. Fiona chose it and told me it would shimmer under the lighting.

"And that one," Darcy said, pointing at my dress, "is so Norah."

I laughed. I couldn't imagine any dress seeming natural on me. "How so?" I asked.

Darcy smiled. "It looks like it's made of stardust."

My mom dropped Darcy and me off at school. As we walked toward the gymnasium door, anxiety hit me like a wall of cold water. Somewhere in there was Zane, waiting for me. And suddenly a thousand questions shot through my head.

Do I go in and search for him? Or stand somewhere and wait for him to find me? Are we just dancing to one or two slow songs or should we hang out all night?

Uncertainty drove me crazy. This was my first dance; I had no idea what I was doing!

"Hey, stress ball," Darcy said, nudging me with her shoulder. "Chill out. Tonight's going to rock."

And with that, she pushed open the door and all my worries evaporated into space.

I'd been there in the gym this afternoon, hanging decorations. But the lights had been on bright, and it hadn't looked like this. Now, with the lights dimmed and everything pulled together . . . the gym had been transformed.

The glow-in-the-dark stars lit up the walls. Shimmering cutouts of planets and moons hung from the ceiling. Glow bracelets dangling from kids' wrists added a cool touch.

Darcy went to get a cup of punch, and I stood peering through the dim light, looking for Zane. I felt a soft tap on my shoulder and turned around with a giant smile.

To face Hunter Fisk.

"Oh, hi, Hunter," I said, trying not to sound disappointed.

"Hey, Norah." He scratched nervously at the back of his head. "Uh, I have to, um, confess something."

Well, this seemed to be the week for confessions. "Okay," I said warily.

His eyes darted back and forth, and he said in a hushed tone, "Slade and I painted that stuff on the dance banner."

" 'The Prom Killer is back'? You wrote that? Why?"

"We wanted to help," he said. "We figured if people thought it was the Prom Killer coming back, that it would take the attention away from Zane."

It had terrified our classmates and nearly gotten the dance canceled altogether, but I guess it was the thought that counted. Hunter and Slade were only trying to help. "Thanks, I guess," I said with a half smile.

But Hunter didn't walk away. He looked down at his shoes and scuffed at the hardwood floor.

"Was there something else?" I prodded.

"Um . . ." A blush rose on his cheeks. "Do you think . . . if I asked Darcy to dance . . . would she say yes or punch me in the face?"

I thought about it for a moment. There had been a few times lately when Darcy seemed a bit . . . funny when the topic of Hunter came up. I grinned. "Go for it, Hunter."

He smiled and dashed off to Darcy's side. I stood still and watched to be sure my instinct was correct.

She didn't punch him.

Fiona was flirting with some cute boy, Maya was having a blast with a few other girls from the Dance Committee, and now Darcy was slow dancing with, of all people, Hunter Fisk. Everyone seemed to be having a great time.

"Excuse me?" said a voice behind me. "Would you like to dance?"

I slowly turned. Zane stood looking totally handsome in khaki pants and a white button-down shirt. And he had his hand out, waiting for mine. For a moment, I thought my heart would explode. But instead I just nodded yes and followed him to the middle of the gym floor.

It had only been a week and a half since I'd last seen him, but it seemed like forever. And now we were about to dance. I'd never danced with a boy before. A wave of anxiety rushed over me. *What if I step on his foot? Where do I put my hands? Should we talk? What should I say?*

But then I put my hands on his shoulders. I recognized the song as one of my favorites. We did this sway-shuffle thing that certainly wasn't graceful. But I realized it didn't matter. Zane's smile lit up his whole face, and I'm sure mine matched.

I felt like I was dancing in space, surrounded by stars and planets. It was like something from a beautiful dream, but it was really happening. I thought for a moment about how it had all come so close to not happening. All because of the same problem. Jealousy had nearly ruined my friendship with Darcy. It had caused Helen to become the Prom Killer. And it turned Amanda's feelings for Zane into rage with almost deadly consequences. Jealousy is no good. I vowed to never feel that way about Zane, Darcy, or anyone.

"Are you having a good time?" Zane asked, and his eyes seemed to twinkle like stars themselves.

POISON APPLE BOOKS

The Dead End

This Totally Bites!

Miss Fortune

Now You See Me...

Midnight Howl

Her Evil Twin

Curiosity Killed the Cat

At First Bite

THRILLING. BONE-CHILLING THESE BOOKS HAVE BITE

Suddenly, she gagged. There was a horrible smell coming from somewhere. From outside? A smell like rotting meat. It smelled like . . . death.

The smell couldn't be coming from the animal — it was just a stray in the yard next door, right? But maybe it was sick and needed help. And the flash of glowing eyes must just have been a reflection of light from somewhere, maybe of the moonlight. Steeling herself, she moved back to the window and looked out again.

Becky gazed down into the McNally yard. She scanned the shadows and the patches of moonlit ground, but, whatever the creature had been, it was gone. The smell lingered, although it seemed a little weaker now, and Becky's stomach turned over.

The animal, whatever it was, *had* seen her with its glowing eyes. Becky *knew* it on some level. Wrapping her arms around herself, she shuddered.

Maybe there was a stray cat or lost dog in the McNally yard, as Becky's parents had suggested. She peered down into the patch of the house next door that she could see through her window. The whining was a little louder now, and irregular. Not the sound of the porch swing creaking or a branch rubbing against the house, but definitely some kind of animal. Becky pressed her forehead against the cold window pane, trying to see.

Something moved in the shadows on the other side of the fence.

It was a huddled shape below one of the evergreen trees in the McNally yard. As Becky watched, it moved a little farther into the moonlight.

Was it a cat, after all? It seemed like it might be cat-size, but the shape didn't seem quite right. The tail was too short, the body looked off somehow. It was moving stiffly, not with the smooth glide of a hunting cat.

The animal raised its head and looked right at Becky. Its eyes flashed a sick, glowing yellowish green.

Instinctively, she moved back, away from the window. Had it seen her? Her heart pounded and she felt like she couldn't catch her breath. Panic bubbled inside her.

A ROTTEN APPLE BOOK

Zombie Dog

Clare Hutton

SCHOLASTIC

Something is in the yard next door,
and it's not happy. . . .

READ ON FOR A SNEAK PEEK!

Becky climbed out of bed. The floor was cold against her feet as she moved hesitantly toward the window, following the sound. When she looked out the window, the scene was shadowy, but lit by the full moon.

"Finished it," she said in a voice that sounded like Eeyore from *Winnie the Pooh*.

The painting was, well, black. Completely black to the edges of the canvas.

"Wow!" Sam exclaimed. "That's one of your best!"

Happy moaned. "It's not very good."

Sam turned to Megan. "Picasso had his blue stage. Happy's in a darker phase."

"I call this one *Midnight*," Happy explained.

Megan could see how the title fit. "It's . . . pretty," she said.

"Thanks," Happy muttered, stepping away from the canvas. She pointed to a twin bed on the other side of the room. "That's yours. The mattress is lumpy."

Megan could have guessed which bed was hers. It had white sheets and yellow covers, whereas the other bed . . . all black.

"I'm sure it will be comfortable," Megan said, trying to stay upbeat.

"No," Happy replied. "It won't."

Megan let out a huge sigh. She assured herself everything would be okay. Zach had told her that zombies didn't sleep much, anyway.

"The girls in the dorm room next to yours are mean. Really mean." Sam grimaced as they walked by a purple-painted door decorated with three cutout gold stars. Each star had a name on it: Brooke. Betsy. Brenda.

" 'Zom-Bs,' " Megan read the big letters printed above the names.

"My advice," Sam said, "is to ignore them. Fly under their radar. The Bs are nasty."

Megan thought about Brett's sister, Hailey Hansen, and her gang of mean girls. "Gotcha," Megan told Sam. "I know girls like that at home."

"We all do," Sam said with a sigh.

He knocked on a plain brown wooden door. "Home sweet home."

The girl who answered the door wore a black dress with black shoes and tights. Her hair was dyed black. Her eyeliner was black and so was her eye shadow. Even her lipstick was black. She looked like a vampire, not like someone with zombitus.

"Hey-ya, Happy," Sam said as if the girl's appearance was totally normal. "Do any painting today?"

Happy didn't seem very happy. She sulked across the room and turned an easel to show Sam a fresh canvas.

ROTTEN APPLE BOOKS:
UNEXPECTED. UNFORGETTABLE.
UNDEAD. GET BITTEN!

If you think life at Zombie Academy
is easy, you're dead wrong!

READ ON FOR A SNEAK PEEK!

There's no mystery these sleuths can't solve!

Check out the other books in the spooky, smart series

sleuth or dare

Book One: Partners in Crime

Best friends Norah and Darcy start their very own detective agency, Partners in Crime. Their first case involves a classmate's missing twin sister, and more than a few shocking twists and turns!

Book Two: Sleepover Stakeout

Norah and Darcy help their friend Maya investigate the strange noises she hears in the house when babysitting. But while cracking the case, Norah and Darcy get into a fight that may lead to the end of the agency!

Local friends and kids in town, for being so excited about this series.

And, most of all, thanks to you. Yes, YOU. Without readers there would be no writers. And all these characters would just be stuck in my head with nothing to do.

Acknowledgments

On the professional side, I would like to thank my agent, Scott Miller; my editor, Aimee Friedman; and the Scholastic crew — Lauren Felsenstein, Nikki Mutch, Becky Shapiro, Jackie Hornberger, Tim Hall, and Yaffa Jaskoll. Also props to Erwin Madrid for the incredible cover illustrations.

On the personal end, thanks to:

My friend Josh Plati, for answering all my school questions.

My son, Ryan, for making me laugh and making me proud.

Mike, my parents, and Susan, for listening to all my crazy plot ideas. And for putting up with me when I'm . . . well . . . crazy.

Darcy shook her head. "I can't believe that when we argued, I said Partners in Crime was 'over.' That's ridiculous. We're just too good."

I threw my head back and laughed. "I know," I said. "I'm glad we got back together. And I look forward to our next case!"

"To teamwork," Darcy said, holding her fist out.

"To best friends forever," I said, and bumped it.

My heart fluttered. "I feel like I'm in a fairy tale."

He shook his head and chuckled.

"What?" I asked, feeling my cheeks flush.

Zane turned serious. "I was in a whole lot of trouble and things were looking pretty hopeless. But you were so smart, brave, and determined. You figured out the truth. If this is a fairy tale, Norah Burridge, then *you're* the hero."

I smiled, and my heart felt like it was going to spin out and orbit the room. "The princess saves the prince," I said. "I like it."

After the song ended, Zane offered to go get us punch. Darcy strolled up to me, grinning. "Is it as perfect as you imagined?"

"Even more so," I said breathlessly.

Darcy grinned at me. "Partners in Crime did it again."

I grinned back. We almost hadn't made it this time, in more ways than one. But things were looking up now. Our friendship was stronger than ever. We righted a wrong. And I was so full of pride and happiness. It was one of those evenings where I felt like anything could happen.